It's all about communication, babe

G B

學校沒教的

神回覆

英語

A !!

跟著MP3這樣講才正統！

MP3

曾祥恩◎著

Sell ice to Eskimos!

聽、讀「神回覆」英語寶典
除了聽懂更要會用

學校沒教，但在跨國公司、外商卻極常聽見的「神回覆」英語
別再鴨子聽雷，強裝鎮定地讓大家以為自己其實都懂
卻無形中造成後續溝通上的誤會

136則
絕佳神回覆情境

● 巧妙破冰
● 不再成為「冷場王」
● 英語溝通滿分

作者序 Author's Words

　　最近在新聞上讀到一個數據，近年來出國留學的學生每年都在減少（總數與百分比）。30 年前每年約有5萬人出國，現在只有一萬多一點。除了少子化是一個原因外，本土博碩士班人數卻比 10 多年前多了十幾倍。我相信現在台灣教育比起以前進步很多，所以在台灣進修已經可以滿足許多學生，可是同時我也怕年輕的一代失去往外踏出與冒險的精神。我想如果當年張忠謀沒出國的話，現在也不會有台積電，世界第一的半導體製造廠，或是如果王雪紅沒有出國，我想也不會有 HTC。我是一個平凡人，沒有甚麼能幫助台灣年輕人的地方，這本書其實能提供的也有限。雖然有許多常見的用語，但是如果不去練習也是枉然。我希望這本書能鼓勵年輕人不要因為英文不夠好的關係而放棄出國的機會，英文練習就可以進步。國外的公司有許多值得學習的地方，比如說領導方式、管理方式，還有最重要的團隊合作，都是我們台灣人可以受益的。如果你今天在猶豫要不要出國，我鼓勵你踏出你的 comfort zone and take risk，我相信你會看到一個嶄新的世界！

John, 曾祥恩 7/13/2016

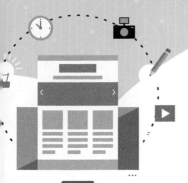

編者序 Editor's Words

　　雖然許多課堂中常談到英語溝通，教科書等也列出許多較理論式的表達，但步入職場或從事口譯工作等後，許多人才像如夢初醒，對英語表達的學習重頭再來過。全書列了在跨國公司、外商公司等常見的對話、慣用語，儘管用字等都平易近人，但也讓許多剛步入跨國、外商公司工作者吃了許多苦頭。

　　其中更包含了有許多用極富趣味性的慣用語，例如 sell ice to Eskimos 等，值得讀者細細品味，這次很榮幸能邀請到中英文俱佳、在國外有多年工作經驗的 John 來編寫這本書，將書中很多情境傳神地描述出來，相信這些對於不管是剛步入職場、求學中，或已步入職場者，在英語口語或口譯上都有許多幫助。

編輯部　敬上

CONTENTS 目次

Part 1 同事：平行溝通零阻礙

1-5 同事閒聊

1-6 離職，另闢職涯新路

Part

2 主管：向上管理有人罩

2-1 舉薦人才

2-2 提案報告

Part

3 主管：向下管理帶人帶心

Part

1

同事：平行溝通零阻礙

　　職場中同事扮演極重要的角色，於步入職場後也近乎是一周相處時間最多的人，了解各種類型同事，並學習怎麼相處是非常重要的，在 part1 中提供 50 情境，無師也能自通。

這根本超過他的負荷了！？
Bite off more than he can chew

情境對話

 MP3 01

John and Peter are chatting in the break room during lunch hour.

John: What happened to Ronald lately? He seems so stressed out.

Peter: He **bites off more than he can chew**, haven't you noticed him staying late at work almost every day?

John: Well, he does have a family of 5 to feed, so I'm sure he's trying his hardest to impress his boss.

Peter: That is right. I heard also that his wife was recently laid off so that probably added fuel to the fire.

John 跟 Peter 午休時在休息室聊天。

John：Ronald 最近怎麼了？他看起來壓力好大。

Peter：他扛太多工作了，你沒發現他每天現在都加班嗎？

John：好吧，他家裡是有五個人要養啦，我想他肯定是利用每一個能表現的機會來讓老闆更賞識自己。

Peter：沒錯，而且我聽説最近他太太剛被開除，這應該更增加了他的動力。

📖 字彙加油站

notice [`notɪs] v. 注意到、提及

impress [ɪm`prɛs] v. 給⋯極深的印象、使⋯銘記

💡 大師提點

　　bite off more than he can chew 的意思是指超過一個人所能承擔的意思，所以在情境中，Ronald 必須要加班才能把手上的事情做完，因為工作量超過他能力所及。而 added fuel on the fire 這個片語就跟我們中文說的火上加油的意思差不多。

加油啊！再撐一會，希望老闆讓你明天晚點進來！？
Hang in there

💬 情境對話

🔘 MP3 02

Mary and Kathy both worked late, as Mary is wrapping up her work she realized she has not eaten dinner yet.

Mary 跟 Kathy 兩個人都在加班，Mary 在快做完她的事情時，突然發現她今晚還沒吃飯。

Mary: Kathy, did you eat dinner yet?

Mary：Kathy，你吃過了嗎？

Kathy: No, I haven't.

Kathy：不，還沒欸。

Mary: Do you want to go grab something together?

Mary：要不要一起去吃個消夜？

Kathy: I wish I could, but I am not seeing myself leaving this place in another hour or so.

Kathy：我很想，但是我起碼要在一個小時才能做完。

Mary: Wow, your manager must be crazy today. Well **hang in there** and hope your boss lets you sleep in tomorrow!

Mary：哇你老闆今天肯定瘋了，加油啊！再撐一會，希望你老闆讓你明天晚點進來。

Kathy：That's not happening...

Kathy：那是不可能的…

📖 字彙加油站

wrap [ræp] *v.* 包、裹、隱藏、使…全神貫注
grab [græb] *vi.* 抓（住），*vt.* 抓取、奪取

💡 大師提點

hang in there 是美國人特別喜歡用的一句話。每當人在困難時期或是很掙扎時，他們就會說 hang in there，就是鼓勵你再撐一下子這樣，情境中 Mary 也鼓勵 Kathy 要再加油，多撐一下。

1

同事：平行溝通零阻礙

2

3

4

我也不知道，好多工作一直湧進來！？
Piling up

💬 情境對話

 MP3 03

> *Ian saw Mark goes in and out of his office constantly.*

Ian: Mark, what is going on? You have been in and out of that door at least a dozen times this morning!

Mark: I don't know Ian, work has been **piling up** nonstop, and I just have to deal with different people at the same time! It's driving me crazy!

Ian: It's driving me crazy to just see you walk in and out of that door!

Ian 看到 Mark 一早一直進出他的辦公室。

Ian：Mark，你到底怎麼啦？你今早起碼進出你的辦公室 10 多次了。

Mark：我也不知道 Ian，好多工作一直湧進來，而我就要同時做很多事，應付很多人。這樣快把我搞瘋了！

Ian：看你這樣一直進進出出才快把我搞瘋了！

📖 字彙加油站

constantly [`kɑnstəntlɪ] *adv.* 不斷地、時常地	
nonstop [nɑn`stɑp] *adv.* 不停地	

💡 大師提點

　　想像一下，辦公桌上的文件越堆越高的感覺。嗯，那就是英文 piling up 的來由來！piling up 字面上就是堆高的意思，而在工作上就形容工作很多應付不來！，情境中，Mark 就因為工作不斷湧入而忙的手忙腳亂的。

💬 情境對話

🔘 MP3 04

" Time is running late and Tina is still working in the office. Collin goes by her cubicle as he is going home "

時間已經很晚了，Tina 仍然在辦公室加班，Collin 下班時經過她的辦公桌。

Collin: It's at the 11th hour, you are still working?

Collin：已經很晚了，還在加班嗎？

Tina: Yeah, there is a proposal due tomorrow, and I want to make sure it is flawless.

Tina：是啊，明天要加一個提案，我希望不要有錯。

Collin: How much longer are you staying?

Collin：你還要多久呢？

Tina: Maybe another 2 hours or so?

Tina：也許兩個多小時吧。

Collin: How about let's go grab dinner first and then you come back and pick up where you left off?

Collin：要不要先一起去吃飯之後，你再回來做？

Tina: Okay, that will do!

Tina：好，這樣也可以！

16

📖 字彙加油站

cubicle [`kjubɪk!] *n.* 小臥室、小隔間	
proposal [prə`poz!] *n.* 建議、計劃、提案	

💡 大師提點

at the 11th hour 意思是已經很晚了，這個詞句也可以用在事情沒做完，時間很趕的時候。比如説「The work is still not done yet? It is already the 11th hour!」。情境中，Collin 也用此表達出已經很晚了，還在加班嗎？來詢問 Tina。

你不知道他們可以私下收回扣嗎！？
Under the table deal

💬 情境對話

 MP3 05

John and Tina are chatting in the break room during lunch hour.

John: Why are our purchasing department colleagues so rich? They drive good cars and dress in name brands.

Tina: You don't know about the popular **"under the table deal?"**

John: Oh! yes but I didn't think they dare to do it. If they get caught isn't that a serious crime?

Tina: It is, but that is why the Bible says greed is the root of all evil.

John 跟 Tina 午休時在休息室聊天。

John：為什麼我們採購部門的同事看起來那麼有錢？他們開好車，衣服也都是名牌。

Tina：你不知道他們可以私下收回扣嗎？

John：我只是沒想到他們這麼大膽。如果被抓到不是很嚴重的罪嗎？

Tina：是很嚴重啊！所以聖經說貪婪乃萬惡之源啊。

📖 字彙加油站

purchase [`pɜtʃəs] *v.* 購買、贏得

colleagues [`kɑlig] *n.* 同事、同行

💡 大師提點

under the table deal 在英文上是指著不在檯面上的協議，不一定是指回扣，而是任何不公開的交易都可以用這詞句，例句中用回扣當翻譯是覺得這在台灣是最普遍的商業行為 under the table deal。情境中，Tina 回覆 John 就是用這句。

對啊，今天過得很不順，我已經累壞！？
Rough day

情境對話

Peter sees John walking to the parking lot ready to go home at the end of the day.

Peter: Hey John, ready to go home?

John: Yes...today's been a **rough one**, and **I'm so out of gas** now.

Peter: I can definitely tell from your face. You must be very happy to go home now.

John: Yes, but the fact that I have to come back early tomorrow makes me sad.

Peter: Well, Friday is only two days away. Cheer up!

John: I will try...

Peter 看到下班時段 John 正在往停車場走過去。

Peter：嘿 John，準備好要回家了嗎？

John：對啊，今天過得很不順，我已經累壞了。

Peter：完全可以從你臉上看出來，不過你可以下班了應該很高興。

John：對啊，但是明天一大早又要回來讓我很難過。

Peter：嗯，在兩天就週末了，加油！

John：我會試試看的…

字彙加油站

rough [rʌf] *adj.* 粗糙的、粗略的

definitely [ˋdɛfənɪtlɪ] *adv.* 明顯地、肯定地

大師提點

　　有在工作一天後趕到筋疲力盡過嗎？相信這是一個很平常的現象。英文中 rough day 就是形容這一天過得不順利，out of gas 在這裡不是形容汽車沒油喔，out of gas 用在人身上就是說一個人筋疲力盡了，像汽車沒汽油一樣！情境中 John 以此表達出今天已經累壞了。

1

同事：平行溝通零阻礙

2

3

4

別打草驚蛇的好！？
Rock the boat

情境對話

MP3 07

"Lawrence has not been assigned to the group that he wants, and he is expressing his concern to Charles."

Lawrence: The project that I'm working on now is not even on the company's priority list. I feel my talent is wasted. I scored so high on last year's evaluation that my manager was thinking to promote me, and I don't understand what I did wrong to get me here.

Charles: Do you think your manager could be jealous of your talent and is thinking to isolate you so your work won't catch too much attention?

Lawrence 沒被分配到他想去的組，他跟 Charles 分享他的想法。

Lawrence：我現在做的項目根本連公司的重視名單都排不上，我覺得我的才能被浪費了。我去年的表現超好，讓我主管甚至考慮要不要給我升官，我不知道我做錯了什麼到今天這地步。

Charles：你的主管有沒有可能在忌妒你的才能，所以想把你邊緣化呢？

Lawrence: Possible, my manager is not exactly the smartest guy and honestly I could overshadow him quite easily.

Charles: Maybe you can talk to him to see what he can do to change your current situation?

Lawrence: Not right now if he is really jealous of me. My pay here is really good, and I don't want to **rock the boat** and give him any excuse to fire me.

Charles: Okay, sounds reasonable.

Lawrence：有可能，我主管不是真的那麼優秀，講實話我可能真的很容易搶走他的鋒頭。

Charles：你要不要跟他談談看，看有沒有機會把你調走？

Lawrence：如果他真的忌妒我那現在可能不是好時機，我薪資在這裡很好，我不想打草驚蛇給他任何理由來開除我。

Charles：好吧，聽起來合理。

字彙加油站

assign [ə`saɪn] *v.* 指派、分配

大師提點

　　雖然我在例句翻譯 rock the boat 是用打草驚蛇，但是兩者還是有一點出入。rock the boat 可以用在任何會改變現狀的情況，可是打草驚蛇感覺一定要是一個對立的角度（人跟蛇的對立），可以説 rock the boat 更通用一些！

23

愛斯基摩人的能力！？
Sell ice to Eskimos

💬 **情境對話**

🔘 MP3 08

Mary and Jack are two top engineers in the company, one day they are having lunch together.

Mary: You know what bothers me the most?

Jack: What is it?

Mary: As important as we are to the company, I can't believe there are sales reps that make more than us.

Jack: Who makes more than us?

Mary: I think Luther makes more than us.

Jack: You know that Luther can **sell ice to Eskimos** right? His selling skill is insane! I'm fine

---

Mary 跟 Jack 是公司的兩名最優秀的工程師，有一天他們一起吃午飯。

Mary：你知道有一件事讓我不舒服嗎？

Jack：什麼事？

Mary：我們對公司這麼重要，竟然還有業務賺得比我們多。

Jack：誰賺得比我們多？

Mary：好像 Luther 賺得比我們多。

Jack：你知道 Luther 有能力賣冰塊給愛斯基摩人吧？他的銷售能力

with him making more than us if he's the only one.

Mary: Yeah....but he is a sales rep!

Jack: I am okay with it. We make the products and he sells them. The company won't be profitable unless both of us are good at our jobs. So I think it is fair.

太強了！他賺得比我多 我一點問題都沒有。

Mary：是沒錯…可是他 是個業務啊！

Jack：我覺得還好，我 們做產品他們銷售。如 果有一方做不好公司都 不能賺錢，所以我覺得 公平。

📖 字彙加油站

profitable [`prɑfɪtəb!] *adj.* 有利的、有益的

💡 大師提點

　　這段例句只是想諷刺一下工程師的心態，很多工程師自以為非常重要，但是公司的確是缺個環節都不行！sell ice to Eskimos 是形容能把東西賣給任何人的能力！愛斯基摩人最不缺的就是冰，但是還買單，就是這個意思！

哈哈…我不想被標註成愛打小報告的人！？
Whistleblower

💬 情境對話

MP3 09

" *Clinton and Frank are noticing Leo using company time to do a lot of his personal work.* "

Clinton 跟 Frank 發現 Leo 用很多公司的時間在做他自己的私事。

Clinton: Leo is on the computer investing stocks all day !

Clinton：Leo 整天都在用電腦搞股票！

Frank: I know! Should we tell the boss about it ?

Frank：對啊！我們要不要去告訴老闆啊？

Clinton: I don't know. I don't want to be labeled as a whistleblower...

Clinton：我不知道。我不是很想被標註為打小報告的人…

Frank: I know, but this is for the good of the company. Maybe we should think twice.

Frank：我知道，但是這對公司好，我們是不是要再想一想？

Clinton: Okay how about we will go tell the boss if Leo still does not correct himself by next week.

Clinton：不然我們再等一個禮拜，如果 Leo 都不改變的話我們就去跟老闆講。

Frank: Sounds good to me.

超版 1 行

Frank：聽起來不錯。

📗 字彙加油站

invest [ɪn`vɛst] *v.* 投資、投入…金錢

label [`leb!] *v.* 把…列為、貼標籤於…

💡 大師提點

　　每個地方都有人愛打小報告，但是相信沒幾個人知道這個字的英文吧！whistleblower 就是在形容這種人！雖然打小報告在中文有一點負面的感覺，英文來說 whistleblower 是挺中立的一個字。因為被告發的對象通常都是做了不誠實或違法的事情。情境中 Clinton 就表明他不是很想被標註為打小報告的人…。

同事：平行溝通零阻礙

1

2

3

4

Scenario 10

動口不動手的人太多了！？
Too many chiefs and not enough Indians

💬 情境對話　　　　　　　　　　🔘 MP3 10

" *Judy is in charge of administration and a lot of times people come to her for help. She is always willing to help, but one day she is fed up and complains to coworker Tina.* "

Judy 負責行政，所以很多時候有人來找她幫忙。她平時都很樂意幫忙，但是有一天她實在受不了，就跟同事 Tina 抱怨。

Judy: Just because I'm in charge of administration does not make me a servant. It seems like everyone can just walk into my office and tell me to do this or that. This company just has **too many chiefs and not enough Indians**！

Judy：就因為我是負責行政的不代表我是他們的僕人。好多時候這幫人隨意就走進我的辦公室，要我做這做那的，這家公司動嘴的人很多，但是做事的人太少了！

Tina: I'm so sorry, did you talk to your boss about it？

Tina：真是抱歉，你有跟老闆提起這件事嗎？

Judy: Yes I did and he said he will assign office assistants to every

Judy：有，他說他會安排每一個部門有自己的

department, so I won't be the only one.

Tina: That sounds like a good plan!

行政同事，就不會一直找我了。

Tina：這聽起來是個好方法！

 字彙加油站

complain [kəm`plen] *v.* 抱怨、訴說病痛

coworker [`ko͵wɝkɚ] *n.* 同事、幫手

大師提點

　　too many chiefs and not enough Indians 意思就是太多會發號施令的隊長，但是做事的手下不夠多！情境中 Judy 表達出心中不滿，就是用這句 too many chiefs and not enough Indians。

唉！剛剛搞砸了一個生意！？
Blow a deal

💬 情境對話　　　　　　　　　　　🔘 MP3 11

" *Frank comes back to office looking frustrated and his colleague Jeff asks him what is wrong.* "

Jeff: Hey! Frank. Why the sad face?

Frank: I just **blew a huge deal** with this company, I was so close, but then they ran a final check on our product quality report and decided not to sign with us.

Jeff: Ouch! What is wrong with the report? Maybe it's not too late to **salvage** the crisis?

Frank: I think it's hard because apparently the inspector described our facility more like

Frank 回辦公室時看起來很沮喪，同事 *Jeff* 問他怎麼了。

Jeff：嘿！Frank，臉色為什麼這麼糟？

Frank：我剛剛搞砸了一個生意，我就差那麼一點點，但是最後他們再看了一次我們的產品質量報告後就決定不簽了。

Jeff：唉呀！那報告有什麼問題嗎？也許我們還有挽救的機會？

Frank：我想有點難，那審核我們的人在報告上說我們的工廠比較像

a lab than manufacturing. That turned them off instantly.	實驗室，不像生產廠房。這一點馬上就讓他們打退堂鼓了。
Jeff: You could invite them to come take a look themselves and maybe they will change their minds.	Jeff：你可以邀請他們自己來看一次啊！也許這會改變他們的想法。
Frank: Yeah, I suppose I can give it a shot. There really is no downside for asking.	Frank：我想也是，反正問一下也沒有壞處。

📖 字彙加油站

salvage [`sælvɪdʒ] *vt.* 拯救、救助

💡 大師提點

　　blow a deal 就是搞砸了一個買賣或生意，salvage 這個單字在商界中挺常出現的。當你想挽救一個產品或計畫時就可以用這個字。情境中 Frank 表達出自己差那麼一點點就搞砸了一個生意，就是用這句。

航空公司竟然這樣亂加價！？
Jack up the price

💬 情境對話

MP3 12

Shirley is going to Japan for a vacation, but she decided last minute and has trouble finding air tickets. She ended up spending 30% more than standard price.

Shirley: I can't believe the airline can just **jack up the price** like that. I have to pay 30% more!

Tiffany: Well next time you'd better plan early. Airlines are evil like that. They know that you have no choice on such a short notice.

Shirley: Yes, I have learned my lesson.

Shirley 要去日本度假，但是她是最後才決定的，所以找不太到機票。她最後付了比平常貴 30% 的錢。

Shirley：我真不敢相信航空公司就這樣亂加價，比平常貴三成！

Tiffany：你下次就要早點計畫，航空公司就是會趁人之危。他們知道你在短時間內沒有選擇，只好付錢。

Shirley：是啊！我學了一課。

📖 字彙加油站

standard [ˋstændəd] *n.* 標準、規範

airline [ˋɛrˏlaɪn] *n.* 航線、航空公司

💡 大師提點

平常要表達出「亂加價」常一時想不出合適的字，而 jack up price 是指那種不合理的亂加價錢的方式。這是很一般的口語，很適合在朋友及同事之間用。老闆面前可能不合適。情境中 Shirley 表達出真不敢相信航空公司就這樣亂加價，比平常貴三成！就用了這個字。

要達到前輩功力是有難度的！？
live up to the expectation

💬 **情境對話**

 MP3 13

> *Anthony is filling in the role for a world renowned scientist Stephen, and is ; therefore, feeling a lot of pressure.*

他來補一位世界有名科學家 Stephen 的缺 Anthony 因此備感壓力。

Anthony: I feel like I can't **live up to the expectation** people put on me. I know I'm not as good as Stephen and there is no way I can produce his results.

Anthony：我覺得我沒有辦法滿足大家對我的期待，我知道我不像 Stephen 那樣出色，而我也沒辦法給出像他那樣的成果。

Darren: Stephen is a rock star in the industry, and I don't think anybody is expecting you to fully replace him. The company just hires you, so Stephen's research can still make progress when he is not around.

Darren：Stephen 在業界是一個明星，而我也不覺得任何人有期待你能完全地取代他。公司找你來是要讓 Stephen 的研究在他不在時還可以繼續。

Anthony: Yes, I know, but when there are things I don't know or

Anthony：是啊，我也知道，但是每當有我不

problems I can't solve people look at me as if they are saying "Why isn't this guy as smart as Stephen?" Their expressions drive me crazy!

Darren: Relax! You just have to accept the fact that you are not as smart as Stephen, and that only puts you in the class of everyone else. You are not stupid or dumb, you graduated from Harvard! You should not have to compare yourself to Stephen!

Anthony: I think you are right. I need to adjust my mentality.

知道的事情或是我解決不了的問題時，我都覺得旁邊的人看我的眼神像在說「為什麼他不像 Stephen 一樣聰明？」那種表情快把我逼瘋了！

Darren：放輕鬆，你只是要接受你不像 Stephen 一樣聰明的事實而已。這不過就把你變得跟其他人一樣。你又不笨，你可是哈佛畢業的高材生！你不需要拿你自己跟 Stephen 來比。

Anthony：我想你是對的，我需要調整我的心態。

📖 字彙加油站

pharmaceutical [ˌfɑrməˋsjutɪk!] *adj.* 藥的、配藥的

💡 大師提點

　　有沒有接過優秀人才的位子呢？通常補位的人要表現得跟前輩一樣出色，新人會有很大的壓力。滿足人家的期待可以用「live up to the expectation」這句詞語。

我能勝任團隊合作阿！？
Team player

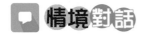 情境對話

MP3 14

Bryan just graduated from college and is preparing for an interview tomorrow. He comes to ask Brandon for interview advice.

Bryan 剛大學畢業，正要準備明天的一個面試，他來問 Brandon 有關面試的意見。

Bryan: How should I prepare for a job interview?

Brandon: Studying some of the common questions asked in an interview helps a lot.

Bryan: How do I make sure that it's an answer they like?

Brandon: There are a couple of things that all companies like to hear during an interview. For example, all companies like to hear that you are a team player and you work well in

Bryan：我要怎麼準備面試呢？

Brandon：找一些很常出現的面試問題，這樣準備很有幫助。

Bryan：我怎麼知道他們想要聽到甚麼答案？

Brandon：許多公司都喜歡聽到一些差不多的答案，比如說所有的公司都喜歡聽你說你是一個以團隊為優先的人，而在任何團隊裡你都可

a team settin. So if they ask you what your strengths are, besides mentioning what you are good at also try to include that you are a good team player.

Bryan:　Okay thanks!

以勝任。所以如果他們問你的強項是甚麼，除了講你專業上的東西，也可以順便提説你是一個以團隊為主的人。

Ｂｒｙａｎ：了解了，謝謝！

📖 字彙加油站

prepare [prɪˋpɛr] v. 準備、為⋯做準備

💡 大師提點

　　如果有一天有想去美國上班的話，一定要記得雖然美國文化有一點個人英雄主義，但是在公司裡是崇尚團隊合作的！在面試時務必要講説你是一個 team player！情境中 Brandon 表達出對面試的看法，表明許多公司都喜歡聽到一些差不多的答案，比如説所有的公司都喜歡聽你説你是一個以團隊為優先的人，就是用這句。

都是些小事情啦！她總是想走捷徑！？
Cut corners

情境對話 MP3 15

" Angela and Laura are talking about Cindy's work ethic. "

Angela 跟 Laura 正在討論 Cindy 的工作態度。

Angela: Cindy's way of doing things bothers me sometimes.

Angela：Cindy 做事的方法讓我有點感冒。

Laura: Really? I don't work with her enough to notice anything. What does she do that bothers you?

Laura：真的啊？我跟她不夠熟，她做了甚麼嗎？

Angela: It's the little things. She always **cuts corners** and tries to do things the fastest way but not necessarily the right way. She doesn't know that it might save her time now, but in the future we might not be able to find the proper data or file.

Angela：都是一些小事情啦，她總是走捷徑想用最快，但不是最正確的方法來處理事情。她不知道雖然現在省了點時間，但是現在沒做好，以後可能會讓公司找不到檔案或數據。

Laura: I see. Did you talk to her about it? After all, she's just an intern. It is good for her if we tell her now to help her career.

Angela: Good idea. I will do it this afternoon.

Laura：我懂了，你有跟她溝通過嗎？她畢竟只是個實習生，現在跟她講對她的未來發展也比較好。

Angela：有道理，那我下午跟她講。

字彙加油站

bother [`baðɚ] *vt.* 打擾、使惱怒、*vi.* 煩惱、擔心

大師提點

　　有沒有跟總是喜歡走捷徑的人共事過呢？英文上就是用 cut corner 這個詞句來形容。如果想說做事很不仔細或丟三落四的可以用 sloppy 這個字。可以這麼說「His work is very sloppy.」。情境中 Angela 小抱怨同事，表示同事總是走捷徑想用最快，但不是最正確的方法來處理事情，就是用這句。

1 同事：平行溝通零阻礙

2

3

4

這筆生意談成的機率看起來不高！？
A long shot

情境對話

MP3 16

" *Linda(sales) and Sean(sales) are on the way back to company from a potential client.* "

Linda: What do you think about that company?

Sean: They are growing fast and by just looking at the office their structure is solid and well-organized.

Linda: I agree, they seem to have all the right elements of a good start-up company, but somehow I don't feel like they like our products too much.

Sean: I don't know about that, I think they try not to show too much interest to give us pressure on

Martin（業務）跟 Sean（業務）剛拜訪完一家公司，在回公司的路上。

Linda：你覺得剛剛那家公司怎麼樣？

Sean：他們成長很快，剛剛看了一下他們辦公室感覺好像也很有制度。

Linda：對啊，一家好的初創公司要有的元素好像他們都有，不過我覺得他們好像對我們的產品不太感興趣。

Sean：我不知道。我認為他們是為了給我們談價上的壓力，才表現

pricing.

Linda: That is true, and they don't seem to be in a hurry to make the decision. Do you think we can get this business?

Sean: I think it's a **long shot**, but definitely possible.

得沒那麼有興趣。

Linda：嗯，他們好像也沒有要那麼快做決定。你覺得我們這筆生意會談成嗎？

Sean：有可能，但是現在看起來機率不高。

📖 字彙加油站

potential [pə`tɛnʃəl] v. 可能、潛能

💡 大師提點

　　a long shot 是美國人常用的一句用語，表示機率不高的意思。字面上是說遠距離打靶那自然機率就低了！情境結尾時，Sean 就表示有可能，但是現在看起來機率不高，機率不高就是用這個片語。

這不是聖誕節，是一年一度的績效考核！？
Performance Evaluation

💬 情境對話 　　　　　　　　　　　🔘 MP3 17

" *Naomi is talking to Belinda and David in the office.* "

Naomi:	Wow it's that time of the year again. Time really does fly.
David:	What time of the year? It's not Christmas yet.
Belinda:	It is not Christmas, but it is the annual **performance evaluation** time....
David:	Oh, no it's that time again huh?
Naomi:	Yes, that means we have to find peer

Naomi 在辦公室跟 *Belinda* 和 *David* 聊天。

Naomi：哇不敢相信又到了那一年一度的時候了耶！時間真的過得好快喔！

David：甚麼一年一度的時候啊！聖誕節還沒到啊！

Belinda：不是聖誕節，是一年一度的績效考核…。

David：喔不會吧！又到這時候了。

Naomi：沒錯，這代表著我們要做同事互相評

evaluation, evaluate ourselves, evaluate our boss, then talk to our boss!

David, Belinda: Yay....

估，評估自己表現、評估老闆，再跟老闆面談！

David, Belinda: 耶…。

📖 字彙加油站

evaluate [ɪ`væljʊˌet] *vt.* 估…的價、對…評價

💡 大師提點

　　年度考核是美國公司一年一度的大事，而這時候員工通常要做很多評估表，雖然加薪令人期待，但是那之前的準備工作是沒有人喜歡的喔！相對的英文詞句就是 performance evaluation。Belinda 回覆 David 時，說了不是聖誕節，是一年一度的績效考核…，就用到這個字。

做事比會說話重要許多！？
actions speak louder than words

💬 情境對話

🔊 MP3 18

" *John and Peter are chatting in the break room at lunch hour.* "

John 跟 Peter 午休時在休息室聊天。

John: What do you think of Alan, the new hire?

John：你覺得新來的 Alan 怎麼樣？

Peter: I haven't really got to know him yet. My first impression is that he's very shy and timid.

Peter：我還沒有機會真的認識他，第一印象是他有點害羞及膽怯吧！

John: I like his work ethic. You know that **actions speak louder than words**. He doesn't talk much, but he shows a lot at his work.

John：我挺欣賞他的工作態度，你知道做事比會說話重要許多，他雖然不太講話，但是他的工作成果很好。

Peter: You are partially right. Nowadays, in order to get noticed by your manager sometimes you still need to effectively express yourself.

Peter：你講對了一半，但是現在的企業，如果要老闆重視你，也需要恰如其分地表達自己。

📖 字彙加油站

impression [ɪmˋprɛʃən] *v.* 印象、影響

💡 大師提點

　　相信你也有認識一些很會耍嘴皮子，但是一旦要動手時就退到後面去的同事，英文 actions speak louder than words 就是形容行動遠遠比講話還重要！此外，在工作後常會遇到做事跟做人哪個重要呢？這個問題，而在情境中 John 回覆我挺欣賞他的工作態度，你知道做事比會説話重要許多，他雖然不太講話，但是他的工作成果很好，就用到這句。

有聽懂嗎 我們從來就沒有共識
On the same page

💬 情境對話　　　　　　　　　　　　　　　🔘 MP3 19

"*Lisa is a new employee, and she's telling Jennifer she is having a hard time working for her boss.*"

Lisa 是一個新的員工，她正在告訴 Jennifer 她不知道怎麼跟老闆共事。

Jennifer: So what exactly is difficult about working for your boss?

Jennifer：所以到底哪裡讓你覺得幫你老闆做事很困難？

Lisa: We can never be **on the same page**, whatever I say he will always interpret it the other way. It's driving me crazy!

Lisa：我們從來沒辦法互相了解，他總是誤解我想要表達的意思。

Jennifer: That is strange. Did you try to talk to him about it?

Jennifer：喔！那真奇怪，你有試著跟他溝通過這件事嗎？

Lisa: I tried, but there is really a communication problem between us. Do you think I

Lisa：有啊！但是我們中間就是有溝通上的問題，你覺得我有辦法申

can ask for a transfer?	請調到別的部門嗎？
Jennifer: Yes, you always can, but that it really depends on whether there is an opening in other divisions.	Jennifer：可以啊，可是那也要別的部門有空缺才行。
Lisa: Thanks I will look into it.	Lisa：謝謝，我會找找。

字彙加油站

interpret [ɪn`tɜ-prɪt] *v.* 解釋、說明、詮釋

大師提點

　　美國人很愛用 on the same page 來形容大家是不是有共識及互相了解，我可以在會議解釋完一項題目後問大家「Are we on the same page here?」，這其實也是另一種在問你「有聽懂我剛剛講的話嗎？」的說法。情境中，Lisa 表示自己跟老闆的問題時，表達出我們從來沒辦法互相了解，他總是誤解我想要表達的意思，就用到這句。

她搞砸了，所以我們現在要付 45%而非 30%！？
Dropped the ball

情境對話

MP3 20

" *Lewis and Clark are chatting during lunch break.* "

Lewis 跟 Clark 在午休時聊天。

Lewis: Why does Francine look so sad this morning?

Lewis：為什麼 Francine 今天看起來很難過啊？

Clark: Oh you haven't heard about it? Remember she was in charge of this company acquisition? She really **dropped the ball** on this one.

Clark：喔！你還沒聽說嗎？記不記得她是負責購買這一家公司的人？她在這過程中犯大錯了。

Lewis: So what exactly happened?

Lewis：所以到底發生甚麼事？

Clark: Well what happened was that this company made a slight adjustment to the payment method, and Francine did not catch it. Now instead of paying them with 30% cash we have to pay 45% cash which is a

Clark：她沒發現那家公司在購買條款上動了手腳，所以我們現在要付對方 45%的現金而不是原來的 30%。老闆很不高興呢！

big deal. The boss was very upset!

Lewis: Oh, yes I bet.

Lewis：喔！那是肯定的。

📖 字彙加油站

acquisition [͵ækwəˋzɪʃən] *v.* 獲得、取得

💡 大師提點

　　dropped the ball 不像是英文的 fail，也不像是 mistake，比較像是中文的搞砸了！另一個更常聽到，但是比較不好在正式場面上用的是 screw up。私下你可以講説「Oh I really screwed up!」。情境中，Clark 回應 Lewis 時説：喔！你還沒聽説嗎？記不記得她是負責購買這一家公司的人？她在這過程中犯大錯了。就用了這個片語。

我下午要找投資人，
發表公司理念！？
VC

💬 情境對話

🔘 MP3 21

" *Josh is thinking of starting his own company, but he does not have an investor yet. This morning his friend Luke walked into his room and saw him practicing a speech in front of mirror.* "

Josh 想要自己出來開公司，可是現在還沒找到投資人。今天早上他朋友 Luke 走進他房間看到他在鏡子前面練習演講。

Luke: Hey Josh, what are you doing?

Luke：嘿！Josh，你在幹什麼啊？

Josh: I have an appointment with a **VC** later this afternoon. I'm practicing my **pitch**.

Josh：我今天下午要去找 VC，所以在練習表達我的公司理念。

Luke: I see, how long does it have to be?

Luke：喔！要講多久啊？

Josh: From what I hear the shorter the better, so the hard part is to sound interesting within the short timeframe.

Josh：我聽說是越短越好，但是要在短的時間讓他們聽了就感興趣很難。

Luke: Good luck!　　　　　　　　　　Luke：祝你好運！

字彙加油站

appointment [əˋpɔɪntmənt] *n.* 約會、任命、指派

大師提點

　　有沒有想過要開公司啊？在美國矽谷有許許多多的人每天往 VC（風險投資家）跑，希望可以拿到 funding（投資）。那些有創新想法的人，就要在投資人面前把他們的想法丟(pitch)出來。久而久之現在大家都叫這類的短演講 pitch，甚至許多人給這種 pitch 取名為「elevator's pitch」，因為常常要在一個如坐電梯般短的時間就要把你的想法講清楚！情境中，Josh 就表明我今天下午要去找 VC，所以在練習表達我的公司理念，就用到這詞彙。

你知道開一家新創公司有多燒錢嗎！？
Burn rate

💬 情境對話

🔘 MP3 22

Josh successfully launched his new company and now he realizes how difficult running a start-up is. He is talking to his friend Luke on the phone.

Josh: Oh I feel like there is a million things to do and 24 hours in a day is not enough!

Luke: Well you are working more than 12 hours a day, so I can see that you are really busy.

Josh: The investor is after me on when will I launch my first product and the timeline he expects is just not possible.

Luke: What is the big deal about delaying the launch? Just talk

Josh 成功地開始了他的公司，但是也開始瞭解營運一家新創公司是那麼的困難。他打電話給他朋友 Luke。

Josh：我覺得一天 24 小時根本不夠用，我每天都有做不完的事！

Luke：我看得出你很忙，因為你一天工作超過 12 個小時。

Josh：投資人在盯緊我要趕快把產品推出來，但是他給的時間表根本就不可能達到。

Luke：延後一下有甚麼關係呢？就解釋給他聽

to your investor and explain to him that it's not realistic.

Josh: The thing is he calculated our **burn rate** precisely and gave us just enough money to survive until we can generate income from the new product. If I delayed more than one month I have no money to pay my staff and every other cost.

Luke: Wow this doesn't sound good.

為什麼這個時間表達不到啊？

Josh：他根據他的時間表算準了我們需要用多少錢，然後只給我們夠用的錢到產品推出那時候。如果我遲一個月再推出產品，我可能就沒有足夠的錢付員工跟其它開銷了。

Luke：喔！這聽起來很糟。

字彙加油站

launch [ˋpɝ·tʃəs] *vt.* 開辦、發起、開始從事 *vi.* 開始、積極投入

大師提點

　　每一個新創公司的老闆一定會對 burn rate 這個詞有概念，因為新公司會經歷一段沒有收入只吃投資或貸款的日子，而 burn rate 就是在形容這個銀行的錢燒得多快。其實這個形容非常貼切，因為一開始的時候，公司真的就像在燒錢一樣。情境中，Josh 回應說他根據自己的時間表算準了需要用多少錢等等的，就用到這詞。

只有少數公司能像 google Cash cow

💬 **情境對話**　　　　　　　　　🔘 MP3 23

" Leslie and Lori works in an investment bank and are responsible for potential IPO company valuation. "

Leslie 跟 Lori 在投資銀行上班，他們倆個負責替有可能上市的公司進行價值評估。

Leslie: Hey Lori you should really look at this start-up company. The idea is very innovative, and I think it has a lot of room for growth.

Leslie：嘿！Lori，你應該來看看這家初創公司。他們的想法非常有創意，我覺得他們很有成長空間。

Lori: Many companies have good ideas, but only a few of them can thrive and grow. It takes the right combination of people, products, and timing to market to create a rapid growth company.

Lori：很多公司都有好的想法，但是只有少數可以真的成長。創造一家可以快速成長的公司需要對的人、產品、及市場的時機。

Leslie: Sure, but I think this company's idea is so disruptive that it can

Leslie：當然，但是我覺得這家公司的想法非

become a **cash cow** like Google. Its initial investment is low, but it creates a good platform for mobile users.

常有破壞性,我覺得它可以成為一家像 Google 一樣可以印鈔票的公司。它的前期投資很低,但是卻創造出一個對所有手機用戶都很實用的平台。

Lori: Okay in that case, let me take a look at its portfolio.

Lori:好,那讓我來看看它的檔案。

innovative [ˋɪnoˌvetɪv] *adj.* 創新的

　　cash cow 是從 dairy cow(乳牛)衍發而來的,因為以前乳牛生產牛奶是一個量大而且穩定的資金來源,所以到現代美國人用 cash cow 來形容一家公司的現金流穩定,而且有種不怕威脅的感覺。情境中 Leslie 表示「當然,但是我覺得這家公司的想法非常有破壞性,我覺得它可以成為一家像 Google 一樣可以印鈔票的公司」時就用這個慣用語。

感覺她能當朋友
卻無法共事！？
Lip Service

💬 情境對話

🔘 MP3 24

"*Nicole is complaining to Larry about Ellison. She does not appreciate her work attitude.*"

Nicole 在跟 Larry 抱怨有關 Ellison 的事情，她不喜歡她的工作態度。

Nicole: Ellison does nothing but **lip service**. I never want to work with her again.

Nicole: Ellison 只會動嘴都不做事！我以後不想要再跟她共事了！

Larry: Really? I didn't recall working with her being that miserable.

Larry：真的嗎？我不記得跟她合作那麼糟糕啊？

Nicole: I don't know, maybe she just does that to me? Or maybe she acts differently toward guys.

Nicole：我不知道，也許她是只對我這樣子？或也許她對男生的態度不一樣？

Larry: That could be true. She seems eager for the spotlight, but I think in general she is still a

Larry：那有可能，她是那種想要在舞台燈光下的人。但是我覺得大致

genuine and likable person.

Nicole: I actually thought she was a good person until I worked with her. I guess she's the type that I can be friends with but not coworker!

Larry: That could be!

來講她還算是一個真誠也滿討人喜歡的人。

Nicole：我原本也覺得她是位好人直到我跟她共事，也許她是那種可以跟我當朋友，但是不能一起工作的人吧！

Larry：有可能喔！

字彙加油站

appreciate [əˋpriʃɪˏet] *vt.* 欣賞、感激 *vi.* 土地增值

大師提點

大部分的人都不喜歡只動嘴不動手的人，這種行為在英文叫做 Lip Service。這個詞句的負面意義蠻重的，所以要看情況而用。情境中 Nicole 表示「Ellison 只會動嘴都不做事！我以後不想要再跟她共事了！」，就用到這個慣用語。

這樣是以小博大啦！？
don't over play your hand

🗨 情境對話

🔘 MP3 25

" *A company is asking for discount on a big order. Adam is reluctant to approve the discount because he thinks the client is satisfied with their quality and is not looking around for alternative sources. However, Eve thinks otherwise.* **"**

一個客戶希望在他們下的大訂單上能有優惠，但是 Adam 不太願意，因為他覺得客人對他們的品質很滿意，所以也沒有再找另外的貨源，Eve 卻沒有那麼樂觀。

Eve: I'm sure they will not be a long term customer if we ignore their request.

Eve：我相信如果我們不搭理他們的要求，他們就不會成為一個長期客戶。

Adam: They know we are the best in the business plus if we let them negotiate this time what about next time?

Adam：他們知道我們是業界最好的，而且如果這次我們答應了，那下次是不是又要再砍一次價？

Eve: I understand, but I want you to

Eve：我了解，我只是

consider the situation carefully and don't **over play your hand**. The customers always have a choice, if we don't handle this properly.

Adam: Okay, maybe you are right.

希望你能考慮得周詳一點，而不要太過自信。客戶總是有選擇的。

Adam：好吧！你説的也有道理。

1

同事：平行溝通零阻礙

2

3

4

字彙加油站

discount [`dɪskaʊnt] *n.* 折扣、不全信

大師提點

overplay your hand 是從撲克牌的用語轉到一般用語的。他的意思是對自己手上的牌（情況）太過自信而做出風險太大的決定（在賭局中就是以小博大最後輸錢）。情境中 Eve 表示「我了解，我只是希望你能考慮得周詳一點，而不要太過自信。客戶總是有選擇的。」時就用到這個片語。

比較這兩種車型，就像是比較蘋果和柳橙一樣！？
They are like apples and oranges

情境對話

MP3 26

Christopher is an intern car salesman, and he is taking a training seminar for how to properly answer customer's questions.

Christopher 是一個實習汽車銷售員，他在上一堂如何回應客戶問題的課程。

Trainer: Remember, never value one type of car over another one. For example, if the customer asks whether a sports car is better than a Sedan. Do not pick a choice but instead say both have their strong suits.

Trainer：記住永遠不要把一種車子說得比另外一種好。就像如果客人問跑車好還是房車好，不要做一個選擇，要說各有好壞。

Christopher: Can you give an example on how exactly you would answer that question?

Christopher：能不能示範一下實際上你會怎麼說？

Trainer: Sure, I can say something like comparing these two

Trainer：可以，我可以說比較這兩種車型就像

types of cars are **comparing apples and oranges** because it depends on the users' need. Sedans are more family oriented, and Sports cars obviously are for drivers with enthusiasm for styles.

Christopher: Okay, thank you.

是比較蘋果跟橘子,主觀成分比較重。房車是比較適合家庭開的,而跑車比較受喜歡有個性及潮流的人歡迎。

Christopher:好,謝謝。

 字彙加油站

properly [`prapɚlɪ] *adv.* 適當地

 大師提點

當美國人在用比較兩種不太能比的東西時,他們喜歡用 they are like apples and oranges 來形容,因為蘋果跟橘子都是水果,但是喜歡哪一種是主觀的選擇。情境中,Trainer 要解釋房車跟跑車哪個好時說「可以,我可以說比較這兩種車型就像是比較蘋果跟橘子,主觀成分比較重。」就用了這句。

他真的不喜歡什麼都說好的人！？
Yes-man

💬 情境對話　　　　　　　　　　　　◉ MP3 27

" *Johnny and Kathy are having a coffee break at a nearby Starbucks* "

Johnny: How long have you been in the company now?

Kathy: Just a little over a year.

Johnny: Nice, time is flying by I kept on thinking you only joined us for a couple of months, how do you like the company?

Kathy: I like it, especially the working environment; my group members are all very friendly and nice. We always have fun and that helps a lot.

Johnny: I bet, is Ian (Kathy's leader) a good person to work for?

Johnny 跟 Kathy 在附近的 Starbucks 喝咖啡休息一下。

Johnny：你來公司多久了啊？

Kathy：超過一年一點點。

Johnny：啊！真的啊！時間過得真快，我一直還以為你才來幾個月呢！還喜歡這裡嗎？

Kathy：我很喜歡，特別是我的團隊每一個人都很好，每天上班都很好玩，而這對我的幫助很大。

Johnny：　　太好了，在 Ian（Kathy 的主

管）下面做事容易嗎？

Kathy: He is, he doesn't like **yes-men**; therefore, it encourages us to speak our true mind.

Johnny: That's great!

Kathy：嗯，他不喜歡大家都只聽他的，所以這樣有做到鼓勵我們講真話的效果。

Johnny：太棒了！

📖 字彙加油站

encourage [ɪnˈkɝɪdʒ] *vt.* 鼓勵、支持、促進

💡 大師提點

　　Yes-man 是在形容那種老闆說甚麼都說好的人，一般來說美國公司不喜歡這種人，他們鼓勵你表達你真實的想法，所以在講 Yes-man 的時候有一點點負面的感覺，但是這在亞洲卻不一定，所以要看場合用囉！情境中 Kathy 回覆「嗯，他不喜歡大家都只聽他的，所以這樣有做到鼓勵我們講真話的效果。」就用到這句。

先看看是不是輸入參數給錯了！？
Garbage in, Garbage out

💬 情境對話

🔘 MP3 23

Daniel (engineer) and Kim (engineer) is discussing a problem together.

Daniel: Why is the simulation output so odd?

Kim: Well, let's trouble shoot to see if there are any mistakes along the way.

Daniel: Let's check the input parameter first, so we avoid any typical **garbage in, garbage out** phenomenon.

Kim: That's a great way to start! The numbers look okay, but I think the range is too wide, so the system cannot recognize.

Daniel（工程師）跟Tom（工程師）正在討論一個問題。

Daniel：為什麼這個模擬結果看起來這麼奇怪？

Kim：嗯，我們來看看是不是過程中做錯了什麼。

Daniel：先看看是不是輸入參數給錯了，不然就會是典型的「垃圾進，垃圾出」的問題。

Kim：這是一個很好的起點！數字看起來還可以，但是範圍有點大，可能系統沒辦法看懂。

Daniel: Okay let's try different combinations and see if it gives a more reasonable result.

Daniel：那我們來試試不同的範圍來看看。

📖 字彙加油站

simulation [ˌsɪmjəˈleʃən] *n.* 模擬、模仿

💡 大師提點

Garbage in, Garbage out 是一句常用的俚語，意思是如果一開始就給錯東西，那過程再好，出來的都是錯的！情境中 Daniel 説「先看看是不是輸入參數給錯了，不然就會是典型的「垃圾進，垃圾出」的問題」，就用到這慣用語。

1

同事：平行溝通零阻礙

2

3

4

不能跟你說唉！
不然你會搶走這稱號！？
Meeting someone halfway

💬 情境對話

 MP3 29

"*Ryan is known as most likable employees in the company. Everyone likes to work with him and regard him as the best teammate to have. Larry wants to know his secret of success.*"

Ryan 是公司裡大家最喜歡的員工，每一個人都喜歡和他合作，也稱他為最好的隊友，Larry 想知道使他成功的秘訣。

Larry: Hey, Ryan what is your secret for being such a good team member?

Ryan: I can't tell you or else you will steal my title.

Larry: Come on, seriously?

Ryan: Of course not, I was just joking. My secret for being such a good team member is **meeting**

Larry：嘿 Ryan，你成為最好團隊隊友的秘訣是什麼？

Ryan：我不能講耶，不然你就會把這個稱號搶走了。

Larry：拜託，你不會是認真的吧？

Ryan：當然不是，剛剛是開玩笑的。我的秘訣就是不管跟誰合作我

everyone halfway no matter who I work with.

Larry: Can you be a little more specific?

Ryan: Compromise is the answer. It does not mean I always let other people push me around. It means to listen carefully to what everyone is saying and move on with a solution that everyone can accept.

Larry: Wow that sounds deep.

都會學習妥協。

Larry：你可以講得再仔細一點嗎？

Ryan：就是妥協。妥協不是就只是聽別人的意見而沒有自己的堅持，妥協是仔細聽完每個人的想法以後，再找到一個每一個人都可以接受的方案。

Larry：哇！聽起來好深奧。

1

同事：平行溝通零阻礙

2

3

4

📖 字彙加油站

likeable [`laɪkəb!] *adj.* 可愛的

💡 大師提點

妥協一般人都喜歡用 compromise 這個單字。meeting someone halfway 表達得會更貼切一點，因為他是說雙方都往前走在中間點會面。這樣的表達方式會更有畫面喔！情境中，Ryan 說「當然不是，剛剛是開玩笑的。我的秘訣就是不管跟誰合作我都會學習妥協」就用到這慣用語。

那我們要不要加一些串場節目來維持氣氛！？
Play it by ear

💬 **情境對話**

> *Sherry and Lucy are responsible for planning for a company event next week. They are in a meeting now to discuss the details.*

Sherry: We need to space out the programs a little better this way, if we run late on several programs we could still end on time.

Lucy: Sounds good, but should we add some fillers in between major programs to keep the atmosphere going?

Sherry: Yes, we don't necessarily have to plan for anything but just **play it by ear** at that time and see what little game or program might work.

Sherry 跟 Lucy 要負責下週公司的一個活動，她們在開會討論細節。

Sherry：我們需要把節目排開一點，這樣要是有些節目太長，我們還是可以準時結束。

Lucy：聽起來不錯，但是我們要不要加一些小的串場節目來維持氣氛？

Sherry：可以啊！我們不用真的準備什麼，就到時候看看現場狀況，我們再來決定要玩個遊戲或是穿插什麼節目。

📖 字彙加油站

atmosphere [`ætməsˌfɪr] *n.* 氣氛、情趣、魅力

💡 大師提點

　　play by ear 就是看狀況在決定要做什麼。你也可以用 improvise 或是 spontaneous。這些字都可以代表就是看狀況而定。你可以説「I will improvise.」或「I will just be spontaneous based on what is there.」。情境中 Sherry 回覆「可以啊！我們不用真的準備什麼，就到時候看看現場狀況，我們再來決定要玩個遊戲或是穿插什麼節目。」時就用到這慣用語。

別怕熱臉貼冷屁股，
把罪惡感拿掉！？
Cold call

💬 情境對話　　　　　　　　　　　　　⭕ MP3 31

" *Lenny is learning to be a sales but he struggles in the first month. He comes to Gordon for help.* "

Lenny 正在學習如何成為一位好的業務，可是第一個月非常不順利。他來找 Gordon 幫忙。

Lenny: Gordon, I have been struggling reaching my sales quota. Can you give me any pointers on how to improve?

Gordon: What area do you struggle with the most?

Lenny: I can't **make cold calls**. I have yet get customers to sign a deal with me over the phone.

Gordon: Yeah so that's a problem. Are you intimidated by the person on the other end of line because 95% of those

Lenny：Gordon，我一直在掙扎達不到銷售目標。你可不可以幫助我進步？

Gordon：你哪方面最有困難？

Lenny：我不知道怎麼打銷售電話，我到現在還沒有成功在電話上跟客戶簽約過。

Gordon：嗯！那是一個問題。你有沒有因為95%的人都討厭接到銷售電話這件事，而害怕

| | people hate getting cold calls? | 面對電話那一頭的人呢？ |

Lenny: Yes, I am always afraid and feel bad I am interrupting their lives!

Lenny：有啊！我總是很害怕，而且我會因為覺得打擾了他們生活，而有罪惡感。

Gordon: Okay! let's start working on getting rid of the guilt!

Gordon：好吧！那第一件事就是要把這個罪惡感拿掉！

字彙加油站

intimidate [ɪnˋtɪməˌdet] *vt.* 威嚇、脅迫

大師提點

　　銷售對許多人都是很困難的，而要常常跟陌生人推銷可能就是最具挑戰性的一部分。英文稱呼這種銷售電話叫做 cold call，我覺得形容得很恰當，因為有一點熱臉貼冷屁股的感覺！Lenny 說明自己的問題時說「我不知道怎麼打銷售電話，我到現在還沒有成功在電話上跟客戶簽約過。」，就用到這慣用語。

他們只是要估一個數字而已，算個大概吧！？
Ballpark

💬 情境對話 MP3 32

" Gerald is giving a presentation to executives. While the meeting is still going on, he rushed out and grab Sherry to go in with him. "

Gerald 正在給主管們做一個報告，會議還進行到一半時，他衝出去還抓 Sherry 跟他一起回去會議。

Sherry: What are you doing? I don't have anything to present!

Sherry：你在幹嘛啊？我又沒有東西要報告！

Gerald: They are asking for some detailed numbers. I got all my numbers from you and you have to help me out now.

Gerald：他們再問一些比較細的數字，我所有的數字都是你給的，所以你要幫幫我。

Sherry: Everything I know is in your presentation. If they want more, I can't help!

Sherry：我已經把我所有的數字給你了，如果他們要更多我沒辦法幫忙！

Gerald: They are only asking for **ballpark numbers**, so just reason out a good estimate

Gerald：他們只是要估一個數字，只要推算出一個大概的就可以了。

and they will take it. They understand we are doing this on the fly, so it doesn't have to be a precise number.

Sherry: Okay, I will try.

他們知道我們是臨時做得，不會要求很精準。

Sherry：好吧！我試試看。

字彙加油站

precise [prɪ`saɪs] *adj.* 精確的

大師提點

　　ballpark 是一個很實用的單字。不管你是做哪一行的都很容易要用到一個大概的數字。你可以跟別人說「I just want a ballpark number.」，或是如果你想要很精確，你也可以說「Don't give me a ballpark number, I need a precise number.」。情境中，Gerald 説「他們只是要估一個數字，只要推算出一個大概的就可以了。他們知道我們是臨時做得，不會要求很精準。」就用到這個字。

1

同事：平行溝通零阻礙

2

3

4

73

不行，我們不能作假帳！？
Cook the books

情境對話

MP3 33

"*At year end company accountants Flora and Eunice are reviewing company's financial statements and notice they are missing a lot of documents.*"

Flora: We have to file these statements tomorrow. Let's just make up some documents to support what we claim.

Eunice: No we can't **cook the books**. If the auditors find out that we played with numbers, the company is going down. Let's **play by the book** and tell them we will make up the missing documents in the future.

Flora: Okay then but first we have to let the boss know.

年底，公司會計 Flora 跟 Eunice 在審核完公司財務報表後發現缺少許多資料檔案。

Flora：明天就要申報了，我們就做一些假的資料來輔助財務報表的申明好了。

Eunice：不行我們不能做假帳。如果查帳的發現我們有造假，公司就完了。我們還是照規矩來跟他們說缺少的資料以後再補齊。

Flora：好，但是讓我們先跟老闆講。

📖 字彙加油站

document ［`dɑkjəmənt］ *n.* 公文、文件、單據

💡 大師提點

　　作假帳在英文裡有個俚語叫 cook the book。book 在這裡就代表了帳簿，然後是被修改過的。play by the book 意思是照規矩來，可以把他想成是照表操課的感覺。情境中，Eunice 說「不行我們不能做假帳。如果查帳的發現我們有造假，公司就完了。我們還是照規矩來跟他們說缺少的資料以後再補齊。」時就用了這兩個慣用語。

我想以這想法…但卻不知道該如何開始！？
Get the ball rolling

💬 **情境對話**

🔘 MP3 34

Starting a business requires knowledge in many areas. Amanda has an excellent idea but does not know how to start a company in practical steps. She comes to her friend Benson for help, who is a very experienced entrepreneur.

Amanda: I have this idea that I want to build around, but I don't know how to **get the ball rolling**!

Benson: Yes, starting a business is not as easy as you think. You need to write a good business plan to start. While you are writing the plan it will force you to think about a lot of things you have not

開始自己的公司需要很多不同方面的知識，Amanda 有一個很好的想法可是不知道實際上的步驟要怎麼走。她來找很有經驗的創業者 Benson 幫忙。

Amanda：我想要以我的這個想法為基礎來開公司，可是我不知道怎麼開始！

Benson：是啊，開一家公司不是那麼簡單的。你需要寫一份商業計畫，在寫計畫的同時會逼你去想一些你還沒想的事情。

thought of before.

Amanda: Can you help me with the plan?

Benson: I can give you the ones I did with my old business. Try to follow my train of thought.

Amanda: Okay. Thank you!

Amanda：你能幫我一起寫計畫嗎？

Benson：我可以給妳我以前的檔案，試著用相同邏輯寫看看。

Amanda：好，謝謝！

 字彙加油站

excellent [ˋɛks!̩nt] *adj.* 傑出的、出色的

大師提點

　　get the ball rolling 就是啟動一項工作，跟之前講過的 jump the gun, get it started 類似。這些詞句都可以換著用，也非常普遍。情境中 Amanda 說「我想要以我的這個想法為基礎來開公司，可是我不知道怎麼開始！」就是用這個慣用語。

繼續待著，順利的話 **50** 歲就能退休！？

Climb up the corporate ladder

💬 **情境對話**　　　　　　　　🔘 MP3 35

" At age 35 Andrew is thinking about making a change in his career. He comes to talk to his mentor Philip for advice. "

35 歲的他在想做一個事業上的改變，所以他來找他的輔導 Philip 詢問意見。

Andrew: I'm in a dilemma. I know staying in the company and continuing to **climb up the corporate ladder** is a low risk move and can guarantee my retirement at age 65. But I have been thinking what if I cannot live that long? Do I really want to spend all the days of my life working?

Philip: If you quit your job what are you going to do?

Andrew：我現在有點困惑。我知道如果我繼續待在公司慢慢往上爬的話是一調相對來說風險比較小的路，而且我到 65 歲時肯定能退休。但是我最近開始想，要是我活不到這麼久怎麼辦？我真的要花這麼多時間在工作上嗎？

Philip：如果你離職的話你要做什麼？

Andrew: I have been thinking to start my own business. If everything goes according to my plan, I can retire when I am 50 and hopefully I still have some time to enjoy my retirement life.

Philip: I tend to tell others that starting a business is not about risk, it is about passion. Don't start a business if early retirement is what drives you, but do start a business you love even if the risk is high.

Andrew: I get it. I will go back and ponder a little more.

Andrew：我在想要開一家自己的公司？如果順利的話，我 50 歲就能退休，這樣的話我還能享受一下退休生活。

Philip：我一般都跟人建議要不要創業不是從風險的角度去考量，而是要從熱情的角度。如果提早退休是你的動力的話，那就不要創業，但是如果你創業要做的事是你所愛的，那也不要因為風險高就停止。

Andrew：我明白了，我會再考慮一下的。

字彙加油站

guarantee [ˌgærən`ti] *v.* 保障、擔保、保證

大師提點

通常一般人如果穩定地待在公司慢慢往上爬我，們稱這種行為「climb up the corporate ladder」，在這裡 ladder 就是梯子的意思，所以白話的講就是順著公司梯子往上爬。

哈哈，你是想拍他馬屁嗎！？
Brownie points

💬 情境對話　　　　　　　　　　　🔘 MP3 36

❝ *Diana is a new secretary in the company. She is trying to figure out how to deal with her boss as he is quite a complicated person. She brings this to colleague Miranda's attention.* ❞

Diana 是新上任的秘書，她還在摸索要怎麼跟她的老闆相處，因為老闆是一個比較複雜的人。她請教她同事 Miranda 這個問題。

Diana: I'm trying to make my boss like me more. What should I do?

Miranda: Are you trying to get some **brownie points**?

Diana: No not at all! I just hope we can have a natural conversation, so it's not that awkward in the office. Honestly, I never see him smile.

Diana：我想要讓我老闆更喜歡我一點，我應該怎麼做？

Miranda：你是想拍他馬屁嗎？

Diana：不是的！我只是希望可以跟他有比較自然的對話，這樣在辦公室裡的氣氛就不會那麼尷尬。講實在的，我從來沒看他笑過。

Miranda: Everybody is different. You are a person that emphasizes relationships, so this might feel awkward for you, but maybe for him this is pretty natural. At the end of the day, as long as you do a good job at work, he will recognize your effort.

Diana: Okay, I see. Thanks for the advice!

Miranda：每一個人都不太一樣。你是一個注重關係的人，所以現在這相處模式可能對你有點奇怪，但是可能你老闆很習慣這種方式。總之我覺得，只要你好好努力工作，老闆還是會肯定你的。

Diana：好的，我了解了，謝謝你的意見。

 字彙加油站

complicated [ˋkɑmpləˌketɪd] *adj.* 複雜的

 大師提點

brownie points 是特意地對老師或老闆好，想加深他們對你的好印象。一般來說以美國人的心理，這就跟拍馬屁有一點類似。情境中 Miranda 回應說「你是想拍他馬屁嗎？」就是用這慣用語。

將心比心思考，
才可以事半功倍！？
Do's and Don'ts

💬 情境對話

● MP3 37

"Kim has over 20 years of experience in selling cars. He noticed the new employee Brandon has trouble selling cars and decides to offer him some advice."

Kim: Hey Brandon, let me tell you some **do's and don'ts** of selling a car.

Brandon: Okay.

Kim: First and foremost is never make a **hard sell**. I saw you do that a couple of times and usually that drives customers away. I know you are anxious to sell your first car but you have to **walk in the customer's shoes**. They won't buy the car from

Kim 有超過 20 年的汽車銷售經驗，而他注意到新來的 Brandon 一直賣不出車子，決定給他一些意見。

Kim：嘿！Brandon，讓我跟你講一些賣車應該做和不該做的。

Brandon：好的。

Kim：第一也是最重要的就是不要逼顧客給他們壓力。我看到你做了幾次這樣的事情，而這樣通常都會把顧客趕走。我知道你很希望趕快賣掉你的第一台車，但是你要以顧客的心態去想。他們不會跟一個

you if they don't like you. Think about it, you are not the only dealer here. They can buy from numerous other locations. The key is to appeal to them like you are on their side. Understand?

Brandon: Yeah I think I tried too hard and it backfired.

他們不喜歡的人買車子,想想看你又不是這裡唯一一會賣車子的,他們有許多選擇。重點就是,你要讓他們喜歡你,也讓他們覺得你是站在他們那一邊的,懂嗎?

Brandon:嗯,我想我做得過頭,反而造成反效果了。

📖 字彙加油站

backfire [`bæk`faɪr] *v.* 失敗、事與願違

💡 大師提點

　　Do's and Don'ts 就是應該做與不應該做的事情。這是一個滿好用的短語。hard sell 就是一種給顧客強硬態度的銷售方式,通常這樣講的時候都是帶有負面的講法。walk in someone's shoe 字面上的意思是穿著別人的鞋子走走看,實際上的意思是要以別人的角度去看以及思考。

給全現金嗎？
那屋主肯定很難拒絕！？
Fall through the cracks

💬 **情境對話**　　　　　　　　　　　　　　　🔘 MP3 38

" Linda is chatting with Angela about her recent house purchase during a coffee break. "

Linda 在下午休息時間起 Angela 她最近買房子的事情。

Linda: Hi Angela, I remember you were bidding on a house last week right? How did it go?

Angela: Don't even talk about it anymore. It was such a perfect fit for my family, but it **fell through the cracks**. Another buyer came in with all the cash and took the house.

Linda: Wow all cash? That must be hard for the owner to resist.

Angela: Yeah and now I have to start looking again.

Linda：嗨！Angela，我記得你上禮拜去投標一個房子對不對？現在怎麼樣呢？

Angela：唉！別提了，那真是一棟適合我家庭的房子，但是沒談成。有人來用全現金買走了。

Linda：全現金？那屋主肯定很難拒絕。

Angela：是啊！所以現在我又要開始找房子了。

字彙加油站

purchase [`pɝtʃəs] *v.* 購買、贏得

大師提點

　　失敗一般人都會用 fail 這個單字來講，但是偶爾在談話中老外喜歡用 fall through the crack 來形容失敗的交易或項目。沒有特別的時機或狀況，一般來說都可以用。情境中，「Angela: 唉！別提了，那真是一棟適合我家庭的房子，但是沒談成。」就用到這個慣用語。

我們老闆居然能身兼數職，也太厲害了！？
Wear many hats

💬 情境對話　　　　　　　　　　　🔘 MP3 39

" *Tommy is a busy man as he runs his own company and at the same time volunteers for many charity organizations. His employees Sonia and Tony admire his stamina.* "

Tony: I don't know how our boss can **wear so many hats**. He is amazing.

Sonia: Seriously! Have you counted how many titles he has? He's the CEO of this company, he is also the chairman of Love To Give charity, not to mention that he is a broad member of five major publicly traded companies!

Tony: Yeah and please don't forget he is a father of three. I bet

Tomm 是一個忙碌的公司老闆，但他同時也在許多慈善機構服務。他的員工 Sonia 跟 Tony 非常敬佩他的精力。

Tony：我不知道我們老闆怎麼可以這樣身兼數職，他太厲害了。

Sonia：真的！你有沒有算過他有多少頭銜？他是這家公司的執行長，他同時也是 Love to Give 慈善機構的負責人，還不說他是 5 家上市公司的董事會員！

Tony：是啊，也別忘記他有三個小孩，我猜他

you he doesn't have any personal time. | 都沒有自己的時間了。

Sonia: I just hope that his body can keep up with all those demands. | Sonia：我只希望他的身體可以撐得住。

📖 字彙加油站

admire [əd`maɪr] *vt.* 欽佩、欣賞

💡 大師提點

　　有一些人天生就可以身兼數職，英文形容這樣有多重身分的人就叫 wear many hats。這句話通常是帶有稱讚性質的，就是說一個人很厲害，可以做不同的事。情境中 Tony 說「我不知道我們老闆怎麼可以這樣身兼數職，他太厲害了。」就用到這個慣用語。

小心謹慎點好，
別讓他逮到機會罵我們！？
Stay on your toes

💬 **情境對話**

🔘 MP3 40

" *Anna and Audrey are chatting during office break, their boss George rushes into the office looking angry* "

Anna 跟 Audrey 在辦公室休息時間聊天，突然看到老闆 George 怒氣沖沖地走進來。

Anna: Uh oh, it looks like George is not in a good mood today. We'd better **stay on our toes** and not give him any excuse to yell at us.

Anna：糟糕，看起來 George 今天心情很不好，我們最好小心點不要給他抓到機會來罵我們。

Audrey: Yes, I remember last time when he vented on Jessie and that was not a pleasant scene.

Audrey：是啊！上次他發洩在 Jessie 身上，實在不是一個好景象。

Anna: Let's just get back to work now.

Anna：我們還是回去工作吧！

Audrey: Good idea

Audrey：好主意。

字彙加油站

rush [rʌʃ] *vi.* 衝、奔、倉促行動， *vt.* 倉促行動、催促

vent [vɛnt] *vt.* 洩漏、發洩感情、排出

大師提點

　　stay on your toes 就好像是躡手躡腳地走路一樣(walking on your toes)，意思是要小心謹慎。在情境中，Anna 回應 George 説「糟糕，看起來 George 今天心情很不好，我們最好小心點不要給他抓到機會來罵我們。」就是用這慣用語。

Scenario 41

還是有東西要趕阿，也不是他不在我就不用做事！？
slack off

📑 情境對話

🔘 MP3 41

" *Manager just left to take a vacation and Landry is already feeling less pressure in the office. Martha comes to his cubicle to chat* "

Martha: How are you doing with the boss on vacation?

Landry: I'm already feeling weights lifted off my shoulders. I don't know why that is because deadlines are still there, and it's not like I can **slack off** and not do any work when he's not around.

Martha: Haha yes it is probably just a psychological reason.

主管剛離開去度假，*Landry* 就已經感覺壓力少了很多。*Martha* 來到他的辦公桌聊天。

Martha：老闆度假你過得怎麼樣啊？

Landry：我已經覺得壓力少了好多。我不知道為什麼，因為還是有趕在截止日前完工啊！也不是說他不在，我就真的可以偷懶不做事情。

Martha：哈哈，對啊大概是心理因素吧！

字彙加油站

pressure [ˋprɛʃɚ] *vt.* 壓、按、擠

deadline [ˋdɛd͵laɪn] *n.* 截止日期

大師提點

　　一般人學英文可能會覺得偷懶是用 lazy 這個字。可是其實 lazy 比較像是在說一個人的性格，像是懶惰，而不是偷懶這種一次性的行為。通常我們叫偷懶 slack off，不是很正式但是同事之間可能也常常會用到。情境中，Landry 說「我已經覺得壓力少了好多。我不知道為什麼，因為還是有趕在截止日前完工啊！也不是說他不在，我就真的可以偷懶不做事情。」就是用到這慣用語。

董事會有接受他的想法和方向嗎！？
Buy-in

💬 **情境對話**

🔘 MP3 42

" *A new CEO is hired to bring company out of the slump. Stan and Lenny are talking about some of the changes the new CEO is implementing.* "

一個新的執行長剛上任來挽救公司的情況。Stan 跟 Lenny 在講新執行長做的一些改變。

Stan: Wow our new boss sure is radical, he cut 10% of the staff on the first day!

Stan：哇！我們的新老闆真是激進，上任第一天就砍掉 10% 的員工。

Lenny: Yeah because he is changing the direction of the company, and therefore he is getting rid of some departments, but I'm sure he will hire new ones for new products.

Lenny：是啊，因為他要改變公司的方向，所以有一些舊的部門他就會要砍掉，但是我相信馬上就會招人來做新產品。

Stan: Do you think the board **buys-in** to his concept and direction?

Stan：你覺得董事會有接受他的想法跟方向嗎？

Lenny: I am not sure, but since he's the CEO now the board will give him his freedom to do what he thinks is right for the company.

Lenny：我不確定，但是既然他已經是執行長了，我想董事們會給他所需要的自由來做他覺得是對公司好的事情。

📖 字彙加油站

implement [ˋɪmpləmənt] *n.* 工具、器具、裝備

radical[ˋrædɪk!] *adj.* 與生俱來的、基本的

💡 大師提點

buy-in 是接受跟相信的意思，在一般對話中跟 believe 一樣常用。但是 buy-in 比較有點傾向於接受。比如說如果一個人演講完，有人問你覺得講員的邏輯分析有沒有道理，我會說 Yeah I buy-in what he said，而不會說 I believe what he said。情境中，Stan 說「你覺得董事會有接受他的想法跟方向嗎？」就是用到這句。

Scenario 43

這種行銷手法就是老鼠會！？
Pyramid scheme

💬 情境對話

" Monica is persuading Amy to join a direct sale business as a side job. It is a new health product and early birds receive great compensation. "

Monica 在說服 Amy 參加一個直銷健康產品的副業。早參與的業務有很好的待遇。

Monica: I made an additional 3,000 dollars on top of my regular income last month! You should join it too!

Amy: No thanks, I usually avoid these multi-level marketing business models because most of them are **pyramid schemes**.

Monica: Wow, you are right. I had not thought about that. I should be careful.

Amy: Yes if I were you, I would pull

Monica：我上個月除了正常薪資外，又多賺了 3000 美金！你也應該參加！

Amy：謝謝，不過不用了，大部分這種多層次的行銷手法都是老鼠會的運作手法。

Monica：哇！你是對的，我沒想到這點，我應該要小心點。

Amy：對啊！你應該趁

out right now since you
already made some money.

早離開，反正你也賺到
了一些錢。

字彙加油站

receive [rɪ`siv] *vt.* 收到、得到

regular [`rɛgjələ] *adj.* 定期的、經常的

大師提點

老鼠會在台灣應該是耳熟能詳的一種商業手法吧！但是大部分的朋友應該不知道英文怎麼講，以老鼠會這種(multi-level marketing)的方式呈現的 fraud （作假）叫做 pyramid scheme。另外一種只是跟你拿錢，然後跟你說保證多少回報的（非法集資）叫做 Ponzi Scheme。情境中，Amy 回說「謝謝，不過不用了，大部分這種多層次的行銷手法都是老鼠會的運作手法。」就用到這個用慣用語。

好的創意就該支持吧！？
Shotgun approach

💬 **情境對話**

🔊 MP3 44

Company recently changed a CEO and everyone immediately feels the different approach the new CEO is taking. Bob and Chad are sharing their thoughts during a tea break.

公司最近換了執行長之後，每個員工馬上感受到了新老闆的不同，*Bob* 跟 *Chad* 在休息時間分享他們的看法。

Bob: What do you think of this new CEO? How is he different than our old boss?

Chad: Well, our old boss is very dominant and likes to give a very specific direction. This new boss is willing to listen to us and tries to discover good ideas from us.

Bob: Yes, our boss is like Steve Jobs who allocated all of Apple's resources to just make a few products and this new

Bob：你覺得這個新執行長怎麼樣？他跟我們舊老闆有甚麼不一樣？

Chad：嗯，舊老闆個性上比較強勢，很喜歡給一個明確的方向。現在的比較會聽我們的看法來試圖從我們中間挖掘出好的想法。

Bob：對，舊老闆像賈伯斯用蘋果所有的資源就做少數產品，而新老闆像賴瑞配吉一樣用散

guy is like Larry Page who uses a **shotgun approach** in Google to launch all the good ideas they can think of.

Chad: That's a good comparison.

彈槍的方式，只要是好的創意都願意支持。

Chad：這個比喻很不錯。

字彙加油站

immediately [ɪ`midɪɪtlɪ] *adv.* 立即地、立刻地

dominant [`dɑmənənt] *adj.* 佔優勢的、支配的

大師提點

shotgun approach 就像用散彈槍一樣，同時打好幾發子彈來增加成功的機率。這在商業界也是一種做法，所以就取了這個名稱。情境中，Bob 說「對，舊老闆像賈伯斯用蘋果所有的資源就做少數產品，而新老闆像賴瑞配吉一樣用散彈槍的方式，只要是好的創意都願意支持。」就用到這句。

該確定合約有沒有綁其他條件！？
No strings attached

💬 **情境對話**

MP3 45

" Wendy just moved to town and started a new job. She has not found her own place and temporarily staying with relatives. This morning she is excited to share with colleagues that she finally found her own place. "

Wendy: I found a great place with reasonable rent!

Franny: Give me some details.

Wendy: Well, it's a 400 square foot studio located 10 minutes away from downtown.

Franny: How much is the rent?

Wendy: It is $1,100 dollars a month.

Wendy 剛搬到城裡開始新工作。在還沒找到房子前，她住在親戚家裡。今天早上她很興奮地跟同事分享她終於找到房子了。

Wendy：我找到了一個又便宜又好的地方！

Franny：告訴我一些細節。

Wendy：一個 400 平方呎的單人套房，離市中心就 10 分鐘。

Franny：多少錢呢？

Wendy：一個月$1100 美金。

Franny: That is a really good deal. Are you sure there are **no strings attached**? Do you need to pay a higher security deposit?

Wendy: Nope, I looked over the contract carefully and all the terms are normal!

Franny：那真的很便宜，你確定沒有暗中綁一些條件嗎？像是要多付較高額押金那類的。

Wendy：沒有，我把合約仔細地看過了，都是正常的條件！

📖 字彙加油站

reasonable [`riznəb!] *adj.* 合理的、通情達理的、正常的

💡 大師提點

　　no strings attached 意思是沒有多餘的附加條件，有很多表面上好的交易會暗中加一些條款在合約上，所以一般人會問說「Are there any strings attached?」來確認有沒有一些沒發現的條件。情境中 Franny 回說「那真的很便宜，你確定沒有暗中綁一些條件嗎？」就用到這個慣用語。

1 同事：平行溝通零阻礙

2

3

4

Scenario 46

他們講的時候也很認真，不像是開玩笑！？
Mean business

💬 情境對話

> *Christmas is approaching and everyone is ready to take vacation. However, company announces that over the break they will not shut down like they did before, they will require a minimum number of staffs on board to keep operation running.*

聖誕節快到了，每個員工都準備好要放假了。但是今年公司公布不像往常一樣休息，需要一些員工在公司維持營運。

Jane: Did you hear the announcement today? I am afraid my boss will ask me to stay over the break!

Jane：你聽到今天的報告了嗎？我好怕老闆會要我留下來！

Chris: I know, and I think they **mean business** when they announce it.

Chris：對啊！他們講的時候也很認真，不像是開玩笑的。

Jane: Let's just hope that enough volunteers step up.

Jane：我們只能希望有足夠的人自願留守了。

Chris: I highly doubt it. It is Christmas time and everybody has already made plans.

Chris：我很懷疑，這是聖誕節，每個人鐵定都已經有計畫了。

📖 字彙加油站

minimum [`mɪnəməm] *n.* 最小量、最低限度

announcement [ə`naʊnsmənt] *n.* 宣布、通知、通告

💡 大師提點

mean business 跟 serious 很像，就是很認真的態度。在一般用語中可以兩種混著用！情境中 Chris 回應「對啊！他們講的時候也很認真，不像是開玩笑的。」就是用到這句。

趁年輕就試著冒冒險吧！？
Walking on water

💬 情境對話 MP3 47

" *John is an engineer who spent eight years in Silicon Valley. He decides to quit his job and moves back to Asia to pursue a start-up opportunity in China. His friend Nathan tries to talk him out of it.* "

John 是一位在矽谷待了 8 年的工程師。他決定辭職搬回亞洲，在中國加入一個初創公司。他的朋友 Nathan 想要說服他放棄這想法。

Nathan: What don't you have here in the US and why do you want to go back to Asia?

Nathan：你在美國缺乏什麼，讓你想搬回亞洲呢？

John: Life here in the States is good and comfortable. But I want to explore the world while I'm still young. I want to **walk on the water** for once. Even though there is a high possibility that I end up regretting the decision, at the end of the day at least I tried.

John：在美國的生活很好、很舒服，但是我想要趁還年輕探索這個世界，我想要試著走在水面上冒險。雖然我很有可能最後會後悔這個決定，但最起碼我試過了。

Nathan: Okay if you have made up your mind, good luck to you.

Nathan：好吧！如果你已經打定主意了，我就祝你好運吧！

pursue [pɚˋsu] *vt.* 追趕、追捕、追求

大師提點

　　walk on the water 是一個從聖經故事傳下來的用語，耶穌叫彼得走在水上去找他，而彼得也照做了。走在水面上需要的是信心及冒險的勇氣，所以當有時候人看不到前方的路或是在冒險的時候可以說 I'm walking on the water。在情境中 John 回應「在美國的生活很好、很舒服，但是我想要趁還年輕探索這個世界，我想要試著走在水面上冒險。」就是用到這句。

同事：平行溝通零阻礙

1

2

3

4

我今天早上被炒了！？
Pink slip

💬 **情境對話**

" *Elsie walks passed Patty's desk and saw her putting her belongings in a Box.* "

Elsie 經過 Patty 的位子時，發現她在收拾她的東西。

Elsie: Patty, why are you putting away your stuff?

Elsie：Patty，你為什麼要收拾妳的東西呢？

Patty: I got a **pink slip** this morning...

Patty：我今天早上被炒了…

Elsie: Oh no! Are you okay?

Elsie：喔！不，那你還好嗎？

Patty: Yeah, I will take a short vacation first before I start looking for the next job.

Patty：嗯，我會先放自己一個假，等回來再找下一份工作。

Elsie: Did Ted (Patty's manager) say why?

Elsie：Ted（Patty 的主管）有沒有説為什麼呢？

Patty: He said it is nothing personal, but my group is cutting costs

Patty：他説跟我沒什麼關係，只是我的團隊要

and because I'm the newest member so...

Elsie: I will ask around to see if there are any openings!

Patty: Okay, thanks!

縮小,既然我是最後加入的,要走的就是我囉…

Elsie:我會到處問問看看有沒有公司在找人!

Patty:好的,謝謝!

📖 字彙加油站

belongings [bə`lɔŋɪŋz] *n.* 財產、攜帶物品

💡 大師提點

早期美國公司在請員工走路時都會放 pink slip 在桌子上,雖然現在這個傳統已經不再,但是口語上我們還是會用 pink slip 代表著被炒魷魚喔!在情境中,Patty 回應 Elsie 時說「我今天早上被炒了…」就是説這句。

找自己所熱愛的工作做吧！？
Nothing ventured, nothing gained

情境對話

MP3 49

" *Angela is thinking about quitting her job and starting her own business. Her colleague William is trying to talk her out of it.* "

William: You have a job that is better than most people. The pay is good, and you don't work over time. What else are you asking for?

Angela: Have you heard of the phrase "**Nothing ventured, nothing gained**?" I need to take a risk to get what I really want. Yes, I have a good job, but I am not passionate about it. If I don't enjoy a job now how can I do it for another 20 years? Steve Jobs said the

Angela 在考慮要離職來開自己的公司，她的同事 William 試著要說服她放棄這想法。

William：你有一份比大部分人都好的工作，你薪水高又不用加班，你還想要甚麼？

Angela：有沒有聽過「不入虎穴，焉得虎子」？為了得到我要的，我需要冒險。的確，我有一份好的工作，可是我對它沒有熱情。如果我不能享受我的工作，那我又怎麼能再做 20 年？史蒂芬‧

most important thing is to find what you love and that is what I'm going to do.

William: Wow okay then.

賈伯斯説最重要的事就是找到自己所熱愛的，所以我要這麼做。

William：那好吧！

📖 字彙加油站

passionate [`pæʃənɪt] *adj.* 熱情的、激昂的

💡 大師提點

　　No venture, no gain 跟我們中文的「不入虎穴，焉得虎子」的意思一模一樣。在商業中更是常用，因為許多創業都是充滿風險的！情境中，Angela 回應說「有沒有聽過「不入虎穴，焉得虎子」？為了得到我要的，我需要冒險。」就是用到這慣用語。

為了日後好相見，
還是別把關係搞僵！？
Burn the bridge

情境對話

" *Monica is not pleased with her work environment and decides to quit her job. On her last day, Nicole comes to say good bye* "

Monica 不太喜歡她的工作環境，所以決定要離職。在他工作的最後一天，Nicole 過來跟她說再見。

Nicole: Did you finish putting away all your stuffs?

Monica: Almost, I should be done in another 20 minutes.

Nicole: Have you thought about yelling at Terry to his face?

Monica: Yes I did! But I figured the best thing is to not **burn the bridge**.

Nicole: That's a wise thing to do as you never know he might be

Nicole：東西都收拾完了嗎？

Monica：差不多了，我想再 20 分鐘就好了。

Nicole：你有沒有想過去吼 Terry 幾聲再走？

Monica：有啊！可是我想我還是不要把關係搞僵比較好。

Nicole：這樣比較好，誰知道也許你下份工作

your reference for your next job.

的介紹人可能是他呢？

Monica: Yes, it is possible.

Monica：是啊！是有可能。

📖 字彙加油站

reference [ˋrɛfərəns] *n.* 證明人、推薦人

💡 大師提點

　　burn the bridge 通常都是在離職時會用到的一個詞句。如果你 burn the bridge 就是說你在離職時跟上家公司鬧翻了。通常這是不被建議的行為，因為很難說以後還會用到這個人脈！在情境中，Monica 回應說「有啊！可是我想我還是不要把關係搞僵比較好。」就是用到這個慣用語。

主管：向上管理有人罩

與主管相處，想必是令許多職場菜鳥或老鳥都很頭疼的問題，在part2收錄了許多實際發生的情境，對於與主管相處上能提供許多很不一樣的看法。

對啊，他在營運作業上有豐富的經驗！？
Track record

情境對話

MP3 51

" *Nathan (HR Manager) is talking to Eric (head hunter) about a potential candidate of operation manager John that Eric referred.* "

Nathan: How did you get in touch with John?

Eric: I knew John long time ago and when you mentioned to me about this opening. I immediately thought about him. He is the perfect candidate.

Nathan: Why do you think so highly of him?

Eric: John has a strong **track record** on setting up operation structure within

Nathan（人事經理）正在跟 Eric（人力公司人員）講有關 Eric 介紹的營運經理 John。

Nathan：你是怎麼跟 John 聯絡上的呢？

Eric：我認識 John 很久了，這次當你說需要一位人選的時候我馬上想到他。John 絕對是你最好的人選。

Nathan：你為什麼這麼推薦他呢？

Eric: John 在營運作業上有豐富的經驗，不管是初創公司或是有規

both start-ups and large public companies. He knows how to customize the operation to match the uniqueness of the company. He's just the guy you are looking for.

模的大公司他都有做過,而且他非常擅長於根據公司的特色來調整營運模式。

Nathan: Okay, sounds good. Let's set up an interview then.

Nathan:聽起來不錯,那我們就安排一個面試吧。

 字彙加油站

perfect [`pɝˋfɪkt] *adj.* 理想的、完美的

 大師提點

經驗總是所有公司在找人時第一個考慮的,而在英文中一般人可以用 experience,但是也常常聽到 track record,兩者都可以用喔!情境中 Eric 回應說「 John 在營運作業上有豐富的經驗,不管是初創公司或是有規模的大公司他都有做過,而且他非常擅長於根據公司的特色來調整營運模式。」就是用到這個慣用語。

Scenario 52

所以他能有什麼貢獻！？
What can he bring to the table

情境對話

MP3 52

Josh is running his new company and is looking for some experienced software engineers to join him. This morning a headhunter, Lewis, called him and recommended Zack.

Lewis: I think Zack is just the person you are looking for, an experienced software engineer who knows multiple languages.

Josh: **What can he bring to the table** exactly?

Lewis: He knows Java, Python, and has dealt with online shopping platforms with the previous start-up. I think besides skills, you need a person who's been through the start-up phase

Josh 開始了他的新公司，而他需要一些有經驗的軟體工程師。今天早上 Lewis 打電話給他，推薦了 Zack。

Lewis：我相信 Zack 就是你在找的人，一個能寫多種語言又有豐富經驗的軟體工程師。

Josh：所以他到底能做什麼貢獻呢？

Lewis：他可以寫 Java 和 Python，也有跟之前一個初創公司做過網路購物平台。我覺得除了能力外，你也需要一個有走過初創公司的

and can handle the pressure.

路、能承擔這種壓力的人。

Josh: I think you are right. I will schedule to meet with him then.

Josh：我想你是對的。我會約他來談一談。

字彙加油站

handle [ˋhænd!] vt. 處理、對待、經營

大師提點

What can he bring to the table? 是說「他可以貢獻什麼？」的意思。這是很普遍的用法，而也有許多人就直接講「What can he offer?」這兩種說法都很通用！情境中，Josh 回應說「所以他到底能做什麼貢獻呢？」就是用到這慣用語。

這款式一定能讓我們取得領先！？
Ahead of the curve

💬 **情境對話** 　　　　　　　　　🔘 MP3 53

" *Paul (Technical director) is introducing the new smart phone to Kim (CEO).* "

Paul: Kim, you need to take a look at this new smart phone we just built. This will definitely put us **ahead of the curve**!

Kim: Awesome! What is the cost to build it?

Paul: That is the **downside**. Our cost will be 30% higher than before.

Kim: 30%! That will wipe out all our margins! Let's have a meeting with the product and marketing groups and get their opinion on if our new phones can convince

---

Paul（技術總監）正在跟 Kim（執行長）介紹最新的智慧手機。

Paul：Kim，你一定要看一下我們剛研發好的智慧型手機，這一款性能一定會讓我們取得領先的地位。

Kim：太棒了！它的成本是多少呢？

Paul：這就是美中不足的地方，我們的成本比起以往會增加 30%。

Kim：30%！這樣會把我們的利潤都吃掉的！我們要跟產品及行銷部門開會，看看他們認不認為新款手機可以說服

consumers to pay a premium.　｜　消費者花更高的價錢購
　　　　　　　　　　　　　　　　買。

字彙加油站

convince [kən`vɪns] *vt.* 使確信、信服

大師提點

　　ahead of the curve 就是代表著領先競爭對手，也有人用 ahead of the pack，兩種用法都可以！downside 指的是負面或缺點，可以用在說一件事或方案的 downside 是甚麼。情境中 Paul 回應說「Kim，你一定要看一下我們剛研發好的智慧型手機，這一款性能一定會讓我們取得領先的地位。」就用了這個慣用語。

為了長遠競爭力是該增加資本支出！？
Cap-Ex

🗨 情境對話

 MP3 54

" *Tim (CEO) and Amber (CFO) are having a discussion regarding next year's budget.* "

Tim（執行長）跟 Amber（財務長）正在討論明年的預算。

Tim: We need to increase our **Cap-Ex and R&D** budget so that we remain competitive in the future.

Tim：為了讓公司在市場上有長遠的競爭力，我們要增加資本支出跟研發經費。

Amber: The number that you gave is too high and that will cause cash flow problems and put our business **at stake**.

Amber：你給我的預算太高了，這樣很可能造成現金流的問題，讓我們公司陷入風險。

Tim: Okay let's lower the marketing and advertisement budgets to create more room for R&D.

Tim：那就讓我們把行銷跟廣告的經費挪一些出來到研發吧！

Amber: Okay, I will redo the calculation.

Amber：好的，那讓我再重新算一次。

字彙加油站

competitive [kəm`pɛtətɪv] *adj.* 競爭性的

大師提點

　　Cap-Ex 及 R&D 都是在財務預算中常出現的單字。Cap-Ex 是 Capital Expenditure 的縮寫，是資本支出的意思。公司要買資產，例如：設備，就會在這個預算下面。R&D 是 Research and Development，就是研發，還有一個詞句在例句中出現的，at stake，就是有風險的意思喔！在商業用語中 business at stake 會常常出現！情境中，Tim 說「為了讓公司在市場上有長遠的競爭力，我們要增加資本支出跟研發經費。」就是用到這慣用語。

超過了我們預期的 **20%**，但那是因為我們的折扣跟優惠策略！？

bottom line

💬 情境對話

🔘 MP3 55

Amber (CFO) is addressing the company financial report to Tim (CEO).

Amber（財務長）正在跟 Tim（執行長）做財務報告。

Tim: Did we reach our goal on revenue this quarter?

Tim：我們這一季銷售有達到目標嗎？

Amber: We have exceeded our goals by 20%, but that is due in large part to discounts and promotions.

Amber：我們超過了我們預期的 20%，但那是因為我們的折扣跟優惠策略。

Tim: Did the move hurt our **bottom line**?

Tim：有沒有影響到我們的盈利？

Amber: We are still **in the black**, but next quarter is not looking as good as competition gets fierce and; therefore, the discount effect might be diluted.

Amber：我們還是賺錢，可是下一季前景不是很好，因為競爭越來越激烈，也讓折扣策略的效果減低。

Tim： Okay that is fine because next quarter we should have new products come in to provide us the margins that we need.

Tim：沒關係，下一季我們會有新產品上架，新產品會提供我們需要的毛利。

📱 字彙加油站

exceed [ɪk`sid] *vt.* 超過、勝過

💡 大師提點

　　bottom line 在英文中很常聽到，就是最後盈利的意思，他的來由是因為利潤是財務報表的最後一排數字，所以就有了這種用法。in the black 就是代表還賺錢，相對的如果説 in the red 就是赤字，也就是虧錢了。情境中，Amber 説「我們還是賺錢，可是下一季前景不是很好，因為競爭越來越激烈，也讓折扣策略的效果減低。」就用到這慣用語。

2

主管：向上管理有人罩

1

3

4

121

上次你們去拜訪的那家公司有後續嗎！？
Touch base

情境對話

MP3 56

" *Shane (sales manager) is listening to sales report conducted by Martin and Sean.* "

Shane（銷售經理）正在聽 Martin（業務）跟 Sean（業務）做的銷售報告。

Martin: Company Box-a signed a one million NT deal with us over the next 2 years.

Martin: Box-a 公司跟我們簽了一份兩年價值台幣一百萬的合約。

Shane: Okay great, how about the company that you two visited last time. Did you have the chance to **touch base** with them again?

Shane：好，棒極了，上次你們去拜訪的那家公司你們後來還有沒有機跟他們聯絡？

Sean: No, they did not show enough interest, so we put them at the lowest priority. But if you like,

Sean：沒有，因為他們沒有表現得對我們很有興趣的樣子，我們就沒有把他們擺在我們的

we can schedule that this week.

Shane: Yes, if it fits your schedule this week, please touch base with them again. This company is growing fast, and if we build a good relationship with them, the future volume could be substantial.

Martin, Sean: Okay will do.

優先名單上，不過如果你想的話，我們下禮拜可以再去探訪他們。

Shane：嗯，如果你們下週不是太忙就找時間去。因為這家公司成長迅速，如果現在跟他們建立好關係，未來有可能可以拿到大訂單。

Martin, Sean：好的。

字彙加油站

substantial [səb`stænʃəl] *adj.* 實質的、大量的、重要的

大師提點

touch base 是一種在公司裡常用的一種說法，就是聯絡的意思，也有很多人說 connect 基本上有點像中文的「搭上線」！情境中，Shane 回說「好，棒極了，上次你們去拜訪的那家公司你們後來還有沒有機跟他們聯絡？」就是用到這個慣用語。

既然這樣那就繼續保持！？
Stay on top of it

💬 情境對話

🔘 MP3 57

" *In the daily morning meeting, Josh (manufacturing engineer) is reporting recent operation issues to Zack (manager)* "

Josh（生產工程師）在早上的會議中跟 Lisa（主管）報告最近發生的一些問題。

Josh: Inventory of raw materials is running low, but the supplier cannot promise to deliver within our time.

Josh：我們原材料的庫存已經很少了，但是供應商可能沒辦法在我們要求的時間內給我們。

Lisa: What is the problem?

Lisa：是什麼問題呢？

Josh: Their factory had a small fire accident last week, and a lot of products were destroyed.

Josh：他們的工廠上禮拜有一個小火災，燒掉了很多產品。

Lisa: That is the main supplier right? What about the other suppliers? Can they increase their usual production and meet our target?

Lisa：這是最主要的廠家對不對？聯繫一下第二跟第三家廠商，看看他們能不能提高平常的量來滿足我們的需求。

Josh: We never really developed the 2nd and 3rd suppliers as the main supplier was always good until now.

Josh：我們沒有其他的供應商，因為這家直到今天以前一直很穩定。

Lisa: Josh, this was one of the **action items** from last quarter. I can't believe you have not done it. I need you to get **on top of this** right now!

Lisa： Josh，找更多供應商是上一季的結論，我不敢相信你還沒做。你現在趕快去做！

Josh: Okay I'll get right on it.

Josh：好的，我這就去。

1
2

主管：向上管理有人罩

3

4

📖 字彙加油站

supplier [sə`plaɪɚ] *n.* 供應者、供應商

💡 大師提點

之前講的 action items 又出現了！這是在公司中非常容易出現的字喔！get on top of it 是指要員工很積極地做交代的工作，在用這一句時通常會給員工一種急迫性，代表這是老闆現在要你做的第一優先的事情！如果是 stay on top of it 就是說繼續做這件事情或保持在狀況內。比如說如果 Josh 下禮拜回來說有兩家廠商願意做，但是量還要再確定，那 Lisa 就可以說「Good job, stay on top of it.」。

我知道大數據是什麼，請你講重點！？
Cut to the chase

MP3 58

Brian wants to propose a new research project to his boss James.

Brian 想跟他老闆 James 提出一個新的研究項目。

Brian: Hey, James, do you have a minute here? I would like to propose a new research idea to you.

Brian：嘿 James 你有空嗎？我想跟你提一個新的研究計畫。

James: Sure please be as efficient as possible with your pitch.

James：好啊，但請你簡潔有力地講完。

Brian: Okay, as you know there is a growing trend in big data. In case you are not familiar with the big data concept, it is to find useful data that is often overlooked in our everyday world. With computing power improving rapidly, we have the tool....

Brian：你應該清楚最近大數據崛起的趨勢。讓我先解釋一下大數據的概念，大數據就是利用現在強大的電腦運算能力，來統計那些我們過去很容易忽略的數據，現在我們有能力…。

James: I know what big data is, can you please just **cut to the chase**? I am quite busy here.

Brian: Oh! yes my idea is to research on even better compression algorithms to help companies store data even more efficiently in the future.

James: Brilliant, why couldn't you just say so?

James：我知道大數據是什麼，請你講重點。我現在很忙。

Brian：喔！好我的想法是研發更有效率的檔案壓縮法，來幫數公司儲存數據。

James：非常好，你為什麼不能一開始就這樣講？

📖 字彙加油站

algorithm [ˈælgəˌrɪðm] *n.* 算法、演算法、規則系統

💡 大師提點

　　cut to the chase 如果是用在人的身上就是請他講重點。但是如果是用在事情上就是說要專注在重要的事上。比如說我們可以這樣用，「We need to cut to the chase on big project and forget about the little projects that don't make money.」。

簽約好像是綁住自己…但好像為時已晚了！？
That ship has sailed

💬 情境對話

🔊 MP3 59

Emily is trying to talk his manager, Andy, out of signing a deal with this specific client.

Emily 正在說服她的主管 Andy 不要跟這位客戶簽約。

Emily: Andy, I don't think we should agree to the terms they are offering. We are straining ourselves, if we sign with them because we don't have the manpower to take on the next possible more lucrative case.

Emily：Andy，我不覺得他們給的條件很好。我們跟他們簽約只是綁住我們自己，讓我們沒有足夠的人力來接下一個更賺錢的專案。

Andy: I'm sorry Emily, but **that ship has sailed**. We signed the contract with them this morning and I won't risk the company's reputation to change course now.

Andy：對不起 Emily，但是現在討論這件事已經太晚了。我們今天早上已經跟這家公司簽約了，而為了我們公司的形象我也不會在現在毀約。

Emily: I didn't know we had already

Emily：我不知道已經

signed. Let's just focus on doing the work and forget what I said then.

Andy: Thank you for your understanding Emily.

簽約了,那就當我什麼都沒講,專心把這件事做完吧!

Andy: Emily,謝謝你的諒解。

字彙加油站

manpower [ˈmænˌpaʊɚ] *n.* 人力、勞動力

大師提點

如果有些事情是已經發生也不能挽回的,美國人很喜歡用這句「Sorry but the ship has sailed」來形容。基本上就跟中國人講「生米已經煮成熟飯」一樣的用法!在情境中,Andy 説「對不起 Emily,但是現在討論這件事已經太晚了。我們今天早上已經跟這家公司簽約了,而為了我們公司的形象我也不會在現在毀約。」就用了這個慣用語。

主管:向上管理有人罩

1
2
3
4

我覺得自己都在原地踏步，你覺得我的方向對嗎！？
On the right track

情境對話

" *Jerry is struggling to make a major breakthrough in his R&D project, he comes to Jonah, his manager, for help.* "

Jerry 在他研發的項目上有瓶頸沒辦法突破，他找主管 Jonah 幫忙。

Jerry: Jonah, I'm really struggling right now because I have been stuck for the past week. Do you think I'm **on the right track** to tackle this problem? Or should I have adopted the other approach?

Jonah: Don't give up so easily yet, show me where you are stuck and let's see if we can brainstorm and solve the issue. In my honest opinion I think your approach is the right way to go but obviously

Jerry：Jonah，我現在很掙扎，因為過去的一個禮拜我都在原地踏步沒有一點進展，你覺得我的方向是對的嗎？還是我應該採取另一種做法重新來過？

Jonah：別這麼快放棄，讓我看看你在哪裡有問題，我們再一起想想怎麼解決這問題。講實話我覺得你的做法是對的，但是很明顯地我的認同不能代表你能馬

that doesn't guarantee immediate success.

Jerry: Okay, thanks. I just need to be reaffirmed again.

上成功。

Jerry：好的，謝謝。我就是需要在這方面再確認一次。

📱 字彙加油站

brainstorm [`bren͵stɔrm] *n.* 集思廣益、靈機一動

💡 大師提點

on the right track 是一個美國人常用來形容在對的方向上的詞句。如果老闆覺得你的做法有問題，他可以這樣說「 I don't think you are on the right track.」或者如果一切進度都順利老闆會講「 Great, I think we are on the right track.」。在情境中 Jerry 回應說「Jonah，我現在很掙扎，因為過去的一個禮拜我都在原地踏步沒有一點進展，你覺得我的方向是對的嗎？還是我應該採取另一種做法重新來過？」時用到這個慣用語。

1

2

主管：向上管理有人罩

3

4

131

但提案裡提供太少細節和運作的方法吧！？

Nuts and bolts

💬 情境對話

🔘 MP3 61

Vanessa is revising her proposal after being rejected last week. She is bringing in the revised version to her manager Joe today.

Vanessa 的提案上禮拜被拒絕了，她正在準備修改後的版本，稍晚帶去給她的主管 Joe 看。

Joe: I like your idea Vanessa, but the proposal does not include enough **nuts and bolts** which I personally think will determine the success of a plan. I asked you to revise it, but I still don't think it's enough. You need to provide me with more details not just a general idea.

Joe: Vanessa，我很喜歡妳的想法，但是提案裡面提供太少細節跟實際運作的方法。這些資料我個人認為足以決定計劃成不成功。我叫你回去修改但還是覺得不夠。你需要給我更多詳細的資料而不只是大方向。

Vanessa: Okay, I'm sorry for not providing enough information.

Vanessa：好的，抱歉提供得太少。我會回去

	I will add more and get back to you again.	補充完再來找你。
Joe:	Yes, and if you need help please ask Mark to help you. He's a very detailed person and he can tell you what information you are lacking.	Joe：好的，如果你需要幫忙就去找 Mark，他對這種細節的掌握很在行，他可以跟你講你缺少甚麼。

字彙加油站

revise [rɪ`vaɪz] *v.* 校訂、修訂

大師提點

　　nuts and bolts 一般代表著螺絲跟螺絲帽，是組裝東西需要的細節。這個語法後來就被拿來形容一個事情的細節跟實際做法的層面。Joe 說「Vanessa，我很喜歡妳的想法，但是提案裡面提供太少細節跟實際運作的方法。這些資料我個人認為足以決定計劃成不成功。」用到這句。

主管：向上管理有人罩

1
2
3
4

那公司明年就要面臨商品化的過程了唉！？
Commoditize

💬 **情境對話**   MP3 62

Randolph is giving a presentation on next year's company outlook to board of directors and CEO Sherry.

Randolph 正在給執行長 Sherry 及董事會做一個公司明年展望的報告。

Randolph: From this chart, we can see that at the end of this year many competitors are picking up their pace to provide quality wireless chips and therefore we can expect our current products are being **commoditized** going into next year.

Randolph：從這個圖我們可以看出來，在今年年底許多競爭對手已經加速開始提供相當有水準的無線晶片，所以我們可以預期明年開始我們的產品會面臨商品化的一個過程。

Sherry: As far as I know these companies are not making products up to our standard correct?

Sherry：就我所知，其他這些公司還不能做出跟上我們水準的產品不是嗎？

Randolph: Yes, most companies lag behind us at least 2 years in technology. However, there are a lot of clients out there who do not have hard specs and are not asking for high standard chips such that price becomes a strong deciding factor.

Sherry: Okay

Randolph：沒錯，大部分公司在技術上還落後我們起碼 2 年，但是許多客戶沒有很嚴格的要求，所以對他們來説價格是一個重要的因素。

Sherry：了解。

字彙加油站

presentation [ˌprizɛnˈteʃən] *n.* 顯示、呈現、簡報

大師提點

要給 commoditize 一個正確的中文翻譯不太容易，雖然在例句中我是用了商品化這個字（網路上查的），但是我感覺這不太能準確地表達這個字的意思。commodity 就是一般大眾可以買的商品，所以他的形容詞變成「商品化」好像聽起來也沒錯。但是我在這裡要再仔細地描述這個字的意思，因為這在商業界是一個重要的觀念。當一家公司的產品從獨強 (monopoly)到完美競爭(perfect competition)這個過程叫 commoditize。而在這個過程中公司的產品也從可以任意設定價格，到要用價格跟對手競爭，因為在完美競爭的市場中，價格是唯一可以區分產品的條件。

相信他們的潛能還沒發揮吧！？
Scratching the surface

💬 情境對話

MP3 63

" Toby is writing an economic report analyzing Africa's economy. He wants to propose to his boss Ryan that they should start setting up a base there. "

Toby 在寫一份經濟報告分析非洲的經濟，他想要跟他老闆 Ryan 提議在非洲設立一個點。

Toby: Africa's economy improves steadily over the past ten years. Political situations have gotten better, and I think they are only **scratching the surface**. We should move a small part of our operations there and try to build a good reputation.

Toby：非洲在過去十年，經濟每年都穩定地上升，政治環境也改善許多，我相信他們的潛能還沒完全發揮。我們應該在那裡設點來打響名聲。

Ryan: Obviously, Africa has had our attention for a while, but most people have not moved in because of the political environment and corruption. Do you have any good suggestion

Ryan：當然，我們都有注意到非洲的趨勢，但是很多人都沒有動就是因為那裡的政治及貪汙。你有想說怎麼做嗎？

on how to operate?

Toby: We can ask our China branch to think of something since China and Africa have a really good relationship.

Toby：我們可以問我們在中國的分公司，中國跟非洲很友好。

Ryan: Okay, let's do that.

Ryan：很好，那就這樣做。

analyze [ˈæn!ˌaɪz] *vt.* 分析、解析

在形容人或事物還沒完全發揮潛力的時候，可以用 scratching the surface。比如說如果一個員工還在學習，但是很有潛力，你就可以說「He is only scratching the surface, he has real potential.」。

哈哈，遲到總比沒到好，但請你下次還是準時！？
Better late than never

情境對話

Ethan is rushing into the office to attend a morning meeting that he is already 15 minutes late for. Terry (Ethan's manager) and Simon are already having discussions.

Ethan: I am so sorry for showing up late.

Terry: **Better late than never**! But do realize that we are all busy people so it would be great if you can be on time next time.

Ethan: I definitely will and again I'm sorry for today. I promise this won't happen next time.

Simon: It's okay Ethan. We just got started here and let me just recap what we just talked

---

Ethan 正在趕去他已經遲到 15 分鐘的一個早上會議。Terry（Ethan 的主管）已經在跟 Simon 開會了。

Ethan：對不起我遲到了。

Terry：遲到總比沒到好。不過請你下次還是準時，因為我們都挺忙的。

Ethan：我會的，真的對不起。我保證下次絕對不會了。

Simon：Ethan 沒關係，我們也才剛開始而已，讓我把我們剛剛討

about here to get you up to speed.

論的跟你說一下，讓你進入狀況。

字彙加油站

attend [əˋtɛnd] *vt.* 出席、參加

promise [ˋprɑmɪs] *vt.* 承諾、保證， *vi.* 作出保證

大師提點

Better late than never!就是遲到總比不到好！這是一種安慰遲到的人或事的說法！情境中 Terry 回應「遲到總比沒到好。不過請你下次還是準時，因為我們都挺忙的。」用到這句。

Scenario 65

被小孩傳染嗎！
打電話請個病假！？
Calling in sick

💬 **情境對話**

 MP3 65

" Ethan is not feeling well today and decides to tell Terry (manager) that he is calling in sick. "

Ethan 今天不舒服，所以打算跟 Terry（主管）說他想請病假。

Ethan: Hello Terry? This is Ethan. I want to let you know that I'm **not feeling good** today and cannot come into the office.

Ethan：喂，Terry 嗎？我是 Ethan，我想跟你說我今天生病，所以不能去公司了。

Terry: Oh okay what happened? Are you **under the weather**?

Terry：喔！好的，你還好嗎？是感冒嗎？

Ethan: I got it from my kids. They have been sick the past week, and it's my turn.

Ethan：我被小孩傳染了，他們上週生病，現在換我了。

Terry: Well don't worry about the work here, I'll let Simon know that you are sick, and he can share the workload.

Terry：不用擔心公事，我會讓 Simon 幫你分擔。

Ethan: Thanks boss.

Ethan：謝謝老闆。

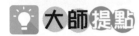

decide [dɪˋsaɪd] *vi. vt.* 決定

大師提點

　　這一篇講到比較多生病時用的詞句，calling in sick 就是打電話請病假，under the weather 就是感冒了（因為天氣冷容易感冒所以叫 under the weather）。

這是份職涯天花板的工作嗎！？
A dead end job

💬 情境對話

> *Alissa has not been very pleased with the advancement of her career. She works for this company for the past ten years and had only been promoted once. She decides to take it to HR Russel.*

Alissa 對自己在公司的升遷不太滿意，她在這裡十年只升遷過一次。她決定跟人事主管 Russel 表態。

Alissa: I don't think the company cares about the individual growth of each employee. I've been here for ten years and not been promoted once even with good evaluations every year. I feel this is a **dead end job**.

Russel: I know you've been working hard, and I'm sorry the company hasn't been able to reward you the way you like. To tell you the truth, you are

Alissa：我不覺得公司有關心我們每一個員工的發展。我在這裡十年了，每年的表現都很好，卻只被升官過一次。我覺得這是一份沒有未來的工作。

Russel：我知道你工作得非常認真，也對公司沒有合理地給予你機會感到抱歉。其實不只是你有這樣的想法，許多

1

2

主管：向上管理有人罩

3

4

not the only one complaining to me about this matter. I am working now to come up with an employee incentive program but please give me a little more time.

其他的員工都有跟我們反應這個問題。我現在有在設計一份員工升遷計畫，但是還需要一些時間來完成，請你再等一下。

Alissa: Okay if the company is working on it already then I am willing to wait. Don't take this the wrong way I have been here for ten years and this place is like a second home to me. But I do also need to cultivate my career.

Alissa：如果公司正視這個問題，那我當然願意等。我在這公司十年了，這裡就像是我的第二個家，但是我也需要為自己的事業盤算。

Russel: That is completely understandable.

Russel：這是能理解的。

📖 字彙加油站

advancement [əd`vænsmənt] *n.* 前進、進展、提高

💡 大師提點

a dead end job 是形容一份沒有任何發展空間的工作，通常意味著做很久卻都做一樣的事，公司也不會給別的機會。

主管：向下管理帶人帶心

　　想必這句超常聽到吧，帶人要帶心説進了許多人的心坎裡，在part3，就帶讀者來看看情境中發生了甚麼事。

在執行上還是有所保留，要在想一下吧！？
Sleep on it

💬 情境對話

🔘 MP3 67

" *Sherry (manager) is reviewing Lennon's new proposal.* **"**

Sherry（經理）在審核 Lennon 的新方案。

Sherry: I like your idea, but there are still some lingering concerns I have about the execution plan. I will have to **sleep on it** to decide if it's really feasible.

Sherry：我蠻喜歡你的想法，不過我對執行上的計劃還有一些保留，所以我需要再想一下這方案的可行性。

Lennon: Okay. Thank you and please let me know what your concerns are because I can always make changes to fit your bill.

Lennon：好的，謝謝。請讓我知道你的考量是什麼，因為我可以修改方案來滿足你的需求。

Sherry: Okay that's great. How about I let you know in another 2 days.

Sherry：很好，那我過兩天讓你知道結果，如何。

Lennon: No problem, I look forward to hearing your feedback.

Lennon：沒問題，我期待你的回覆。

📖字彙加油站

review [rɪˋvju] *vt.* 在檢查、評論、檢閱

💡大師提點

sleep on it 的意思就是要在想一下，有點像是在睡覺也在想的那種感覺！fit the bill 是說符合需求的意思！情境中，Sherry 說「我蠻喜歡你的想法，不過我對執行上的計劃還有一些保留，所以我需要再想一下這方案的可行性。」用到這個慣用語。

3

主管：向下管理帶人帶心

這責任是該誰來擔呢！？
Shoulder the blame

💬 **情境對話**

🔘 MP3 68

" *Linda (Manager), Matt, and Donald are having a meeting regarding a mistake.* "

Linda: What exactly happened?

Matt: We made a wrong assumption on the model and the data that client has is inaccurate.

Linda: So who will **shoulder the blame**?

Donald: I was the one that made the assumption and did not consult with the others. My apologies.

Linda: It's okay. Let's just focus on how to fix this problem. I will

Linda（經理）、Matt 跟 Donald 在開會討論一個錯誤。

Linda：所以到底發生了甚麼事？

Matt：我們所做的數據模型中有錯誤的假設，所以現在客人手上的數據是錯誤的。

Linda：這件事誰要負責呢？

Donald：這是我的錯，是我做這個假設時沒有跟別人討論就擅自做了決定。

Linda：算了，讓我們專心集中在怎麼挽回這

contact the client and in the meantime try your best to fix the data and send it to them.

件事，我來跟客戶連絡，那你們就把握時間趕快把數據修好寄給他們。

字彙加油站

inaccurate [ɪnˋækjərɪt] *adj.* 不正確的

大師提點

shoulder the blame 就是承擔錯誤的意思，一般通常也會聽到「Who is responsible for it?」兩種都可以混著用喔！情境中，Linda 問說「這件事誰要負責呢？」用到這個慣用語。

主管：向下管理帶人帶心

我們的行銷策略是想拉高產品週期！？
Product lifetime

💬 情境對話

" Kate (marketing manager) and Susan are having a discussion on an upcoming new product. "

Kate（行銷經理）跟 Susan 在討論要上架的新產品。

Kate: How long do you expect the **product lifetime** to be?

Kate：這個產品能賣多久呢？

Susan: I would expect it to be about 3-5 years, which is the industry average.

Susan：這個產業的平均產品壽命是 3-5 年。

Kate: Okay, we need to come up with a marketing strategy to stretch the product lifetime to 7 years. We invested 30% more in this product than our previous ones. We need a longer lifetime to compensate for the investment.

Kate：我們需要想出一個行銷策略，將產品的壽命提高到 7 年，我們花在這個產品的投資比之前多了 30%，所以我們要拉長產品壽命來彌補。

字彙加油站

expect [ɪk`spɛkt] *vt.* 期望、期待

大師提點

　　product lifetime 通常代表著產品從上架到下架的時間，行銷中還有一詞叫 product life cycle 是產品週期的意思千萬不要搞混喔！在討論過後，Kate 詢問「這個產品能賣多久呢？」用了這個慣用語。

再降 10%，要打進市場！？
Get your foot in the door

💬 情境對話

🔘 MP3 70

" Kate (marketing manager) and Susan is discussing about the pricing strategy on a product in the new market. "

Kate（行銷經理）跟 Susan 在討論一個產品在新市場的價錢策略。

Kate: We should lower the price more on this product.

Kate：我們的價錢要再低一些。

Susan: The margin on the product is already thin. I'm afraid there is no more room to discount it.

Susan：我們這項產品的利潤已經很薄了，恐怕沒有甚麼折扣的空間。

Kate: The current goal is to **get our foot in the door**, not to make profit. Lower the price by another 10%.

Kate：我們現在的目標不是要賺錢，是要打進市場，再降 10%。

Susan: Okay, I will do that.

Susan：好的，我會這樣做。

🔲 字彙加油站

current [ˋkɝənt] *adj.* 當前的、流行的

💡 大師提點

　　get your foot in the door 在英文上是先不管三七二十一就先擠進門口的意思，常常是在形容狀態還不理想或是不全面時，卻為了先機而來的一種作風。在情境中 Kate 回應 Susan 時說「我們現在的目標不是要賺錢，是要打進市場，再降 10%。」用到這句。

這些計畫都太中規中矩了，在大膽點！？
Think outside the box

💬 情境對話

🔘 MP3 71

"Kim (CEO) is reviewing all the new proposals from R&D group and is ready to feedback to Paul (technical director)"

Kim（執行長）正在審核研發團隊的計畫，也同時要讓 Paul（技術總監）知道他的想法。

Kim: There are a lot of good ideas here, but Paul I'm looking for another major direction.

Kim：這裡面是有許多不錯的想法，可是 Paul 我想要一個全新的方向。

Paul: A major revolution?

Paul：一個全新的產品想法？

Kim: Yes, no more incremental changes that will only give us the edge for half a year, but something revolutionary!

Kim：對！我不要再做那種只能給我們半年優勢的小改變，我要一個會震驚市場的新產品理念！

Paul: So none of the proposals **fit the bill**?

Paul：現在手上的計畫案沒有您滿意的嗎？

Kim: No, all these ideas still **play by the rules**. I want a bold and wild idea. The key is to **think outside the box**.

Paul: I understand. I will get right on it.

Kim：沒有，這些計畫都太中規中矩了，我想要一個更大膽、更瘋狂的點子。重點是要運用想像力打破常規。

Paul：我明白了，我馬上去做。

字彙加油站

incremental [ɪnkrə`mənt!] *adj.* 增加的、增值的

大師提點

　　美國文化非常重視想像力，而其中常常用的詞句就是 be creative，或是 be original。Think outside the box 是其中最高的一種讚美，因為這是一種打破傳統思想的想像力！play by the rule 就是照規矩來，一般來說是好事，但是以想像力來說就是中規中矩，沒有甚麼創新。

3

主管：向下管理帶人帶心

4

來腦力激盪一下。每一個工程師都要寫下五個新想法！？
Going back to the drawing board

💬 **情境對話**　　　　　　　　　　　　　🔊 MP3 72

" *Paul (technical director) is addressing to all the engineers what Tim (CEO) just told him about being creative.* "

Paul: Tim just reviewed our proposals and would like us to come up with more innovative ideas.

Daniel: What is the plan now?

Paul: Now we will go **back to the drawing board** and start **brainstorming**. Each engineer needs to come out with five new ideas, doesn't matter how crazy or unrealistic they sound. Write them down and submit to me by next

Paul（技術總監）正在把 Tim（執行長）剛剛講要更具創新力的意思傳遞給所有工程師。

Paul：Tim 看了我們的計畫方案，他想要我們提出更具創新力的想法。

Daniel：那我們現在應該怎麼做？

Paul：我們現在要重新開始來腦力激盪一下。每一個工程師都要寫下五個新想法，不管聽起來有多不實際或是瘋狂都沒關係。下禮拜前要寄給我，然後我們再開會，團隊評估每個想

week and we will have a meeting to discuss them and do a group evaluation on each idea.

法。

All: Okay.

All：好的。

📖 字彙加油站

submit [səb`mɪt] *vt.* 使服從、使屈服、遞交

💡 大師提點

　　之前提到的 going back to the drawing board 這裡又用到了！這真的是常常出現又實用的詞句。brainstorm 是美國人很喜歡的作法，就是讓每個人不管想到什麼都寫下來，然後最後在挑看看有沒有可以用的 idea。在中文中他就像是腦力激盪的意思，通常都是在團體裡做。外國公司常常這樣做來刺激創意喔！

開完會了，
接下來又是分析報告！？
Action items

💬 情境對話

> *Kate (marketing manager) is having a meeting with Susan and Chelsea.*

Kate（行銷經理）正在跟 Susan 及 Chelsea 開會。

Kate: Okay that's all I have today, Do you two have any questions?

Kate：好了，我講得差不多了，你們兩個有甚麼問題嗎？

Chelsea: No

Chelsea：沒有。

Kate: Can you repeat what the **action items** are again?

Kate：那請把你們回去要做的事再重複一遍。

Susan: I will crunch the numbers on different proposals and see which ones have the best chance to succeed.

Susan：我會把不同提案的數字算出來，看看哪一個比較有機會成功。

Chelsea: I will do a SWOT analysis to see where our company fits in the **competitive landscape**.

Chelsea：我會做一份強弱危機分析報告，來看看我們公司在競爭全景圖的位置。

Kate: Okay that sounds good. Make sure all the report get to me before the week ends.

Kate：好的，請這週末前把報告寄給我。

 **字彙加油站**

propose [prə`poz!] *n.* 建議等的提出、求婚

 **大師提點**

　　action items 是每一個開會一定會用到的詞。他的意思是說開完會後要做的事項，而通常美國公司都很注意這件事，不然他們會覺得開會沒有結論，是浪費時間。competitive landscape 是行銷裡的術語，在形容競爭公司中的一個全景圖表！

加強硬體方面的功能就能夠保持領先嗎！？
Raise the bar

情境對話

> *Paul (technical director) is having a meeting with all the engineers in the company.*

Paul（技術總監）正在跟所有工程師開會。

Paul: Competition is getting fierce in the industry, and there is a downward pressure on price every year. How do we **raise the bar** to stay **ahead of the curve**?

Paul：競爭現在越來越激烈，價錢一直在下降，我們要怎麼做才能保持領先的地位呢？

Daniel: On the hardware side, we know we are improving on processor speed and other functions, but everyone else is doing the same and that is the problem.

Daniel：硬體方面我們的功能一直在加強，像是處理器速度等，可是每家公司都在往這個方向走。

Matt: Software is facing the same problem. It seems that many functions and features are

Matt：軟體也有同樣的問題，每家公司都推出差不多的更新性能。

duplicated across the industry.

Paul: For the next smart phone we will need to provide a big **breakthrough** on top of incremental improvements!

Paul：下一款智慧手機，我們除了要有該有的更新功能外，也要有重大的突破！

字彙加油站

fierce [fɪrs] *adj.* 兇猛的、激烈的

大師提點

ahead of the curve 又出現了！他真的是很常用的詞句！raise the bar 是代表説要提升標準，簡單的説就是要進步。breakthrough 是突破，也是常用的字！在工程師會議後，Paul 回應「競爭現在越來越激烈，價錢一直在下降，我們要怎麼做才能保持領先的地位呢？」時説了這句。

Scenario 75

我不再想聽了，你們私下再討論！？
Take it offline

情境對話

 MP3 75

" Annie and Simon got into an argument on whose proposal is better in front of Terry in the meeting. "

Annie 跟 Simon 為了爭論誰的提案比較好在 Terry 面前吵了起來。

Annie: If we do it your way, we will spend too much time on the product launch and miss out on the opportunity to capture the current market. The market is hot right now!

Ethan：如果按照你的做法花那麼多時間在產品上，那我們就沒辦法馬上賺錢了，現在的市場很旺啊！

Simon: You are a short-sighted as ever! We can gain all that back in the next year and dominate the competitors if we invest the time and energy right now!

Simon：你怎麼可以這麼短視啊，失去的可以在以後賺回來啊！我們現在投資在產品上以後，就可以在競爭對手中取得優勢！

Terry: Okay you two, I don't want to listen to this. Please **take it offline,** and let's move on to

Terry：好了，你們兩個，我不想聽了，你們私下再討論，我們現在

another topic.

要進行下一個討論事項。

📱 字彙加油站

capture [`kæptʃɚ] *v.* 捕獲、引起注意、迷住

💡 大師提點

take it offline 常常在開會中出現，因為很多人常常會在會議中起爭執，而這時候 take it offline 就很好用，因為這就是叫他們私下再講，不要妨礙開會。在情境中，Terry 回應「好了，你們兩個，我不想聽了，你們私下再討論，我們現在要進行下一個討論事項。」時用了這個慣用語。

Scenario 76

去年我們的方向是錯的，改變方向才能重新獲得產品優勢！？

Started off on the wrong foot

💬 情境對話

 MP3 76

" Paul (technical director) is having a brainstorming session with all the engineers "

Paul（技術總監）正在跟所有工程師進行一個腦力激盪的會議。

Paul: Now that we are clear that we **started off on the wrong foot** Last year, we needed to change our course and regain our edge this year. So please think creatively to help the next product design.

Paul：我們現在很清楚去年我們的方向是錯的，我們今年得要改變方向來使我們重新獲得產品優勢。現在請你們發揮想像力來幫助下一個產品的構想。

Daniel: To prevent us from making the same mistake again, what we should do is really focus on what the users will enjoy using, and not just random creative ideas.

Daniel：為了不重蹈覆轍，我們要學習如何從使用者的角度去思考，不是只要是有創意的點子都是好的。

Matt: Daniel made a great point, I think a lot of times our

Matt: Daniel 講得很好，很多時候我們工程

engineers get caught up in what is so called the latest, fastest, or coolest technology, but overlook what users really want.

Paul: Good start. Let's start our session.

師很容易迷上最新、最酷或是最有想像力的發明，可是常常忘記使用者想要甚麼樣的功能。

Paul：很好的開始，請大家開始進行腦力激盪。

📖 字彙加油站

random [`rændəm] *adj.* 隨便的、任意的

💡 大師提點

很多時候我們形容做一件事情一開始沒做好就可以用 started off on the wrong foot。字面上的意思就是好像一開始就走錯腳一樣，這在形容關係或事件都可以通用！在情境中，Paul 回說「我們現在很清楚去年我們的方向是錯的，我們今年得要改變方向來使我們重新獲得產品優勢。現在請你們發揮想像力來幫助下一個產品的構想。」用了這個慣用語。

1

2

3

主管：向下管理帶人帶心

4

時間已經這麼晚了，
我們今天就到這裡吧！？
Let's call it a day

情境對話

MP3 77

Paul (technical director) and all the engineers are continuing the brainstorming session, and it's getting late.

Paul（技術總監）跟所有工程師們正在繼續腦力激盪的會議，而時間也漸漸晚了。

Paul: Anybody wants to share more ideas? If not, can we collect all the shared ideas and discuss the possibility of each?

Paul：還有人要分享更多想法嗎？如果沒有，我們可以針對剛剛講過的想法討論一下可行性。

Tom: From my perspective, I think wireless charging is only useful, if the charging distance can be extended. Short distance wireless charging will not benefit the users that much.

Tom：我覺得無線充電不是很有用，如果充電距離不能再拉長一點。這麼短距離的無線充電不會讓使用者有什麼實質幫助。

Paul: Good point, I just realized the time is pretty late, and let's continue the discussion

Paul：嗯！有道理，我剛剛才發現時間已經這麼晚了，我們今天就到

tomorrow and **call it a day**.

這裡，剩下的明天繼續討論。

📖 字彙加油站

wireless [`waɪrlɪs] *adj.* 無線的

💡 大師提點

開會開到很晚是每一個上班族都一定會經歷過的，而在這漫長的會議中所有員工就是希望聽到老闆說這一句：Let's call it a day 這句英文是說今天就到這裡的意思！在情境中，Paul 回說「嗯！有道理，我剛剛才發現時間已經這麼晚了，我們今天就到這裡，剩下的明天繼續討論。」用了這個慣用語。

💬 情境對話

🔘 MP3 78

" *Kim (CEO) is addressing to all the employees about last year's performance and looking at this year.* "

Kim（執行長）正在跟全體員工做一個年度報告。報告中他回顧去年的表現，也講一下今年的目標。

Kim: So even though last year's performance did not meet our expectations, we still made profit and the promised raises and bonus will still be valid for all of you.

Kim：所以雖然去年我們表現不如預期，但是也還是賺到了錢，所以答應你們的加薪跟獎金公司還是會發。

Paul: Does last year's not so good performance affect this year's Cap-Ex and other potential expenditures?

Paul：去年表現不如預期會不會影響到今年的設備資產支出跟一些其他的支出？

Kim: That is a good question, and the answer is yes. We will go through a time where we have

Kim：這是一個很好的問題，而我會說真的是有影響，我們公司要過

to **tighten our belt** and not spend so much money as a company. But of course if there are categories that you feel investment is a must you can discuss them with me.

一段比較節省的日子，盡量避免不要的花費。但是如果有會幫助公司的投資，讓你覺得是必要的，還是可以來跟我談。

字彙加油站

performance [pəˋfɔrməns] *n.* 演出、演奏、表演

大師提點

2008 年金融海嘯讓所有美國公司都經歷一段比較困難的時期，那時候在公司就很容易聽到這一句 tighten the belt，就是要節省花費。現在全世界進入薄利時代，我想以後聽到的機會是愈來愈多了！在情境中，Kim 回說「這是一個很好的問題，而我會說真的是有影響，我們公司要過一段比較節省的日子，盡量避免不要的花費。但是如果有會幫助公司的投資，讓你覺得是必要的，還是可以來跟我談。」時用了這慣用語。

主管：向下管理帶人帶心

1

2

3

4

直接跟他們說，我們不會再降價了！？
Take the bull by the horns

情境對話

MP3 79

Kate (marketing manager) is talking to Susan about a specific product price negotiation.

Kate（行銷經理）正在跟 Susan 討論其中一樣產品的議價。

Kate: This particular tier-1 company is pressuring us to reduce the price even more. I am loosing negotiation power, but at the same time we really don't have any more room to cut.

Kate：這家大公司再度施壓力給我們，要再把價錢壓低，他們的態度很強硬，但我們真的沒有讓價格再調降的空間了。

Susan: In this particular segment, we have the most competitive pricing already, I say we **take the bull by the horns** and tell them we are not reducing the price.

Susan：在這產業裡我們已經給最優惠的價格了，我建議我們不要再斡旋了，堅持地面對他們，跟他們溝通我們不會再降價了。

Kate: Yes we have the most competitive pricing, but a lot of other companies are watching

Kate：是啊！但是旁邊有很多公司都在等這個能跟他們做生意的機

and waiting for opportunity to do business with them. I'm sure some of them will accept whatever price they ask for just to do business with them.

Susan: That's true, but it's not a sustainable strategy. This company will realize we are the best partner in the long run.

會，這些公司一定會不管價錢先簽約再說。

Susan：這是真的，但這不是長久之計，他們不可能繼續用這麼低的價錢做生意。這樣子這家大公司就會瞭解我們才是最適合的供應商。

字彙加油站

sustainable [sə`stenəb!] *adj.* 支撐得住的、能承受的、可永續發展的

大師提點

take the bull by the horns 在英文字面上是說去抓公牛的角，這應該是一件危險的事情，卻也是正面跟不逃避問題的一種最直接的做法。在例句中這就是我們要表達的，不逃避而且直接面對問題。

3

主管：向下管理帶人帶心

171

有什麼意見能使公司更進步呢！？
Here's my two cents

💬 情境對話

🔘 MP3 80

"Tim (CEO) and other executives are having a meeting."

Tim (執行長) 跟其他主管正在開會。

Tim: Is there any feedback that you would like to make to help improve our company?

Tim：你們有沒有什麼意見可以幫助公司再進步呢？

Eric: **Here's my two cents**, I feel there is room for improvement regarding operation efficiency. I notice that sometimes project managers have only the title but don't have actual authority and power to do many things because none of the team members really report to him or her. They are borrowing people from other groups and therefore the priority sometimes is not there for them.

Eric：我有一個想法，我覺得在公司運作上還有進步的空間，比如說我發現很多時候專案經理只是空有頭銜，但是沒有實質的權力，因為下面的人都是從其他專屬部門借來的。這樣子很多時候都沒有辦法把優先權放在他們的專案上。

Tim: Interesting and valid point, I think you need to communicate with HR and devise a new structure for project manager to make life easier on them. Nathan, can you talk to Eric about this?

Nathan: Yes, Tim I will.

Tim：嗯！很有道理，這一方面你需要跟人事溝通好，以幫助專案經理有新的架構定位來讓他們能更有效率。Nathan，你能不能跟 Eric 討論這件事？

Nathan：好的，Tim。

📖 字彙加油站

efficiency [ɪˋfɪʃənsɪ] *n.* 效率、效能、功效

💡 大師提點

外國人開會通常都很注重每個人發表意見，如果像在亞洲公司那樣都當 Yes man 的話，主管會覺得你不盡心為公司奉獻。所以 Here's my two cents 在外國公司就很常聽到，就是說明這是我的想法的意思，在字面上 two cents 只是兩分錢，也有代表著謙卑的味道，所以在發表自己想法時也不會給人強勢的感覺！

3

主管：向下管理帶人帶心

安排新架構是難…
該咬緊牙關撐過去！？
Bite the bullet

💬 情境對話

MP3 81

Company is facing financial burden, Tim (CEO) is talking to Nathan (HR manager) about restructuring.

公司正在面對財務壓力，Tim（執行長）跟 Nathan（人事經理）在討論設立新的架構。

Tim: We need to restructure our system so that we utilize all our manpower to the best efficiency.

Tim：我們需要一個新的架構，好讓我們可以把每個員工的效率都帶出來。

Nathan: Yes, last time Eric's proposal regarding to the project managers is already underway for change.

Nathan：嗯，上次 Eric 提出有關專案經理的制度調整已經在做改變了。

Tim: That is just one area. Let's look at all the possible improvements we can make with a new structure. I know restructuring is always hard for employees and the

Tim：這只是一部分，我們需要看看每一塊可以改進的地方。我知道安排新架構總是對員工及公司很難，但是讓我們咬緊牙關撐過去，做

company, but let's **bite the bullet** and make this right from the beginning.

一次就到位。

Nathan: Okay, I sure will get on top of this.

Nathan：好的，我會開始執行這件事。

 字彙加油站

restructure [riˋstrʌktʃɚ] v. 改組、重建、調整

 大師提點

bite the bullet 很像我們中文講的咬緊牙關。他的來由是當美國人在打內戰時動手術的過程，因為太痛了所以要咬緊子彈來分心。現在這詞都用在面對困難抉擇或事件時要面對的心態。

未免突發狀況…
我們該在預定時間內完成！？
Land on your feet

💬 情境對話　　　　　　　　　　　　🔘 MP3 82

" In a conference meeting, Shirley is kicking off a new project as she explains the goal and timeline to her team members. "

Shirley: This project is very important to us, and we want to make sure **we land on our feet** and reach all the milestones on time. Any questions?

Ian: The schedule is very tight, if any unexpected things happened then we will not be able to meet this deadline.

Shirley: Yes, I understand; therefore, we need to prepare for anything unexpected.

Shirley 正在會議中啟動一項專案，跟團隊指出項目所需要達到的目標及時間表。

Shirley：這是一個非常重要的項目，所以我們要確定我們能在所有預定的時間上完成目標，大家有沒有問題？

Ian：這個時間表很緊，要是有突發狀況我們沒辦法在這時間內完成。

Shirley：沒錯，我了解所以我們要充分地準備來防止任何突發事故。

字彙加油站

explain[ɪk`splen] *v.* 解釋、說明、闡明

大師提點

　　land on your feet 有點像是在形容一位體操選手，在做完許多高難度動作後最後仍然雙腳著地。英文上也藉著這樣的情景來欲表成功。你可以說，「we need to be successful,」「we want to reach our goals」，也可以說「we want to land on our feet.」。在情境中，Shirley 回說「這是一個非常重要的項目，所以我們要確定我們能在所有預定的時間上完成目標，大家有沒有問題？」用了這個慣用語。

要生存下去，
可是要裁掉不少人！？
Keep your head above water

💬 情境對話

🔘 MP3 83

Companies are facing layoffs in slow economy. Jason, the CEO of Talent Acquisition, is facing a tough decision as he holds a discussion with CFO Jeremy.

許多公司在經濟不好時都面臨裁員，Talent Acquisition 的執行長 Jason 在跟財務長 Jeremy 討論如何面對這個難題。

Jason: How much cost do we need to slash to **keep head above the water**?

Jason：我們要減少多少開銷才能讓公司生存？

Jeremy: We need to reduce operation cost by $460,000 a quarter.

Jeremy：我們每一季需要減少 460,000 元。

Jason: Wow if we reduce all that from staff that's a lot of salaries.

Jason：如果全從員工薪水那邊省的話，是很多人要走的。

Jeremy: Yes but I think we can trim down our cost in some other

Jeremy：對！但是我們還可以從別的方面省

areas, I think we just need to let go 10 people.

Jason: Okay let's hold meeting with all directors to see if we can get a list of people we can terminate.

錢，我估計大概要裁掉 10 個員工。

Jason：好吧！那我們找所有主管來開會，看看能不能列出可裁掉的員工。

📖 字彙加油站

trim [trɪm] *v.* 修剪、整理、調整

💡 大師提點

經濟不好時對許多公司的資金周轉都不容易。很多時候公司只是想要撐過那段冬天，而 keep your head above water 就可能是許多公司為了要生存下去的目標。情境中，Jason 回說「我們要減少多少開銷才能讓公司生存？」時用了這個慣用語。

3 主管：向下管理帶人帶心

現在知道什麼是屋漏偏逢連夜雨了！？

When it rains, it pours

💬 情境對話

🔘 MP3 84

" *As economy slows down, some banks are reluctant to approve loan. Company CEO Jeremy holds an emergency meeting with CFO Richard for alternative funding source.* "

經濟景氣衰退時，許多銀行比較不願意放款。公司執行長 Jeremy 跟財務長 Richard 為了資金來源緊急開會。

Jeremy: If the bank does not approve this loan, then we will definitely run out of cash in 2 months.

Jeremy：如果銀行不放款的話，我們再兩個月就會沒錢了。

Richard: Yes, on top of that I just heard one of the customers cancelled its order due to the slow economy. That will put even more pressure on our cash flow.

Richard：對啊，而且我剛剛聽說有一個客戶因為經濟景氣不好的原因，把訂單取消了。這會加重我們財務的負擔。

Jeremy: Now I know what it means when they say **when it rains, it pours**.

Jeremy：我現在知道什麼是屋漏偏逢連夜雨了。

Richard: Let's just hope for the best.

Richard：我們只能期待最好的事發生。

 字彙加油站

reluctant [rɪˋlʌktənt] *adj.* 不情願的、勉強的

💡 大師提點

　　When it rains, it pours.就是說一下雨就是傾盆大雨。這有一點像是我們講的「屋漏偏逢連夜雨」，但是如果是只有單一重大損失發生時，也可以用這的詞句！在情境中，Jeremy 回說「我現在知道什麼是屋漏偏逢連夜雨了。」用到這個慣用語。

新產品的方向他讓我做主，
嘻嘻！？

Give someone a free hand

情境對話

> *Linda is in charge of the product group and is responsible for introducing new products for next year. She is brainstorming ideas with Ken this afternoon.*

Linda 是產品部門的主管，她負責明年的新產品。今天下午她要跟 Ken 腦力激盪來想一下新企劃。

Ken: Did the boss tell you what direction he wants to go in with the new products?

Ken：老闆有説新產品的方向嗎？

Linda: No. He gave me a **free hand**. We should have a lot of flexibility in terms of new ideas.

Linda：沒有，他讓我來做主，所以我們可以自由發揮。

Ken: Or maybe he's clueless, so he wants us to think of something for him to pick. In that case we'd etter come out with at least 5 proposals, so he can choose one.

Ken：或者他只是沒甚麼想法，所以他要我們想一些來給他選。這樣的話我們最好準備起碼 5 個方案來給他選擇。

Linda: I think you are right. That makes our lives more difficult...

Ken: Difficult indeed...

Linda：你説得有道理，這讓我們更辛苦…。

Ken：的確很辛苦…。

 字彙加油站

direction [dəˋrɛkʃən] *n.* 方向、方位

 大師提點

　　give someone a free hand 就是放手讓人去做的意思，也許更一般在公司的説法是 empowerment，也可以這樣説「My boss empowered me to make my own decision.」。

1

2

3

主管：向下管理帶人帶心

4

183

客人那邊不願意把晶片尺寸放寬一點的話，我們的設計可能得重新來過！？
Go back to the drawing board

情境對話

MP3 86

" *Lisa (technical director) is having a discussion with Daniel (Engineer) and Tom (Engineer).* "

Lisa（技術總監）正在跟 Daniel（工程師）及 Tom 工程師）開會討論。

Lisa: What is the progress on project X-next?

Lisa: X-next 項目進行得怎麼樣？

Daniel: Not great, we have been struggling with the design to incorporate all the functions we want on the chip.

Daniel：不是太好，要把全部需要的功能放在這個晶片上有點難度。

Tom: The bad news is, if we cannot get more relaxing specs from the client on chip size, we might be **going back to the drawing board**.

Tom：壞消息是如果客人那邊不願意把晶片尺寸放寬一點的話，我們的設計可能得重新來過。

Lisa: That is awful. I will try to negotiate with the client to see if they can relax the specs.

Lisa：這聽起來糟透了，讓我來跟客戶那邊交涉看看。

📔 字彙加油站

negotiate [nɪˋgoʃɪˌet] *v.* 談判、協商、洽談

💡 大師提點

go back to the drawing board 是回到起點的意思，也有人用 go back to square one，兩者雖然都可以用，但是 back to square one 比較普遍用在日常生活中，而 back to drawing board 比較像在方案或計畫上用的感覺。

沒有多餘的要求嗎？我不敢相信他們讓我們這麼輕鬆就過關！？
Tradeoff

情境對話

MP3 87

Rita (technical director), Daniel (engineer), and Tom (engineer) are continuing the further discussion on project X-next after Paul contacted the clients.

Rita（技術總監）、Daniel（工程師）和Tom（工程師）在 Paul 跟客戶溝通過了之後，繼續討論項目 X-Next。

Rita: Good news. They relaxed the spec for the chip size by 10%.

Rita：好消息！客戶他們放寬了晶片尺寸 10%。

Daniel: Great, this way we should have no problem finishing the chip design by the due date.

Daniel：太好了！這樣我們就能在預定的日期內設計完了。

Tom: There is no **tradeoff**? I can't believe they let us go that easily. This client is the bully in the industry.

Tom：沒有多餘的要求嗎？我不敢相信他們讓我們這麼輕鬆就過關，這家公司在業界是出名的流氓。

Rita: You got that right. Now we need to finish the design one month before the original deadline and offer another free design change on the previous case.

Tom, Daniel: Oh no....

Paul：你答對了，我們現在不但要比預期的早一個月設計完，也同時要為上次幫他們做的項目做免費設計調整。

Tom, Daniel：噢！不…。

字彙加油站

original [əˋrɪdʒən!] *adj.* 最初的、原始的

大師提點

　　tradeoff 是一個常見的英文單字，意思是要捨取的是什麼，也可以說 What's the catch? 有點像中文的「天下沒有白吃的午餐」的感覺，總是要付點代價吧！在情境中，Tom 回應「沒有多餘的要求嗎？我不敢相信他們讓我們這麼輕鬆就過關，這家公司在業界是出名的流氓。」時用了這個慣用語。

以後這個項目的東西我都要知道！？
Keep someone in the loop

情境對話

 MP3 88

"Paul (technical director) is talking to Daniel (engineer) and Tom (engineer)"

Paul（技術總監）正在跟 Daniel（工程師）及 Tom（工程師）講話。

Paul: On the progress of project X-next, please also **keep Sandy (project manager) in the loop**.

Paul：以後項目 X-next 的進度都要讓 Sandy（項目經理）知道。

Daniel: She is always on our email list, so she should be able to see all our updates.

Daniel: Sandy 一直在我們的 email 清單上啊！所有的對話跟進展她應該都看得到啊。

Paul: Maybe last time when I negotiated with the client I forgot to formalize our new deal in email, so she seems to upset because she is the project manager after all.

Paul：那可能是上次我跟客戶在電話講完後忘記用 email 再重複一次，所以她似乎才會生氣，因為畢竟她是項目經理嘛。

Tom: So we are **off the hook**?

Paul: Yeah, I will apologize to her.

Tom：所以我們沒事囉？

Paul：嗯，我會找時間跟她道歉的。

 字彙加油站

update[ʌpˋdet] *n.* 最新情況

 大師提點

　　keep sb. in the loop 就是讓某人在溝通的管道上。在公司裡不同的部門常常要合作，可能就會讓另一個部門的經理了解狀況，就可以這樣用。off the hook 也是常常用到的詞句，就是中文形容的「逃過一劫」的意思！

1

2

3

主管：向下管理帶人帶心

4

做得比要求的多！？
Go the extra mile

💬 **情境對話**

🔊 MP3 89

" Kim (CEO) is having the annual performance evaluation meeting with Paul (technical director) "

Kim（執行長）正在跟 Paul（技術總監）做一對一的員工評估。

Kim: Well it looks like you are quite modest and don't rate yourself too high on the mark.

Kim：你今年有點謙虛，沒給自己很高分喔？

Paul: I think the reason I did not rate myself as high as I would have liked is because this year's product development is not as successful as I would have liked.

Paul：我也想給自己高分，不過今年的新產品表現沒有很亮眼，所以我給自己比較低一點。

Kim: Your point is valid as this year we have been struggling with new products, but I won't use that to discount your credit because sometimes inspiration cannot be forced. If it doesn't come to you there is not much

Kim：你說得有道理，我們今年的新產品是有點瓶頸，不過我不會用這一點來說你表現不好。靈感這種東西，有時候比較說不準，它不來的時候逼也沒辦法。

you can do. I will give you high remarks on your performance because you always **went the extra mile**. I ask you to do one thing, but you do three. I like your work ethic and your staff also enjoys working with you, that's also very important. Keep up the good work.

Paul: Thank you Kim. I appreciate the kind words.

我給你高分是因為你總是做得比我要求的多，我要你做一件事你回來做了三件。我喜歡你的工作態度，你的員工也喜歡為你做事，繼續保持你的表現。

Paul：謝謝你，Kim。謝謝你的鼓勵。

字彙加油站

valid [`vælɪd] *adj.* 有效的、有根據的、令人信服的

大師提點

　　每一家公司都喜歡做事認真又積極向上的員工，英文 Go the extra mile 可以形容這種員工，因為他們總是做的比被要求的更多！

191

快別擋著公司發財！？
road block

💬 情境對話

🔘 MP3 90

" *Shane (sales manager) is asking about the sales quota progress made by Martin and Sean* "

Shane（銷售經理）正在問 Martin 跟 Sean 的業務進度。

Shane: How are sales progressing? Are you on pace to meet this quarter's target?

Shane：你們業務進度怎麼樣，能不能達到這季的目標？

Martin: We are falling behind a little, and hopefully we will catch up by the end of this month.

Martin：我們現在稍微落後一點，希望這個月底我們可以趕回進度。

Shane: Is there a specific **road block** that's slowing you down? Or just the usual fluctuation?

Shane：有什麼特別攔阻你們的事嗎？還是只是偶爾的銷售不順利？

Sean: We spent a lot of time trying to close the deal with this one company, but this company still hasn't signed and at the same time maybe we lost some other opportunities.

Sean：我們之前花很多時間在這一家公司上，想跟他們簽約。可是他們到現在還沒簽，也因為這樣我們失去了一些別的機會。

Shane: Okay, that doesn't sound too bad. I'm confident you two can meet the target this quarter.	Shane：聽起來沒什麼大問題，我對你們達到這一季的目標有信心。

字彙加油站

progress [prəˋgrɛs] *v.* 前進、進行

大師提點

相信許多人都經歷過上班不順利的事情，通常在公司中一次不順利老闆都不太放在心上，但是如果有一些事情常常出現，老闆就會知道需要改進，有可能是制度上或是人上要改進。這種攔阻公司好好運行的人事物就可以用 road block 來講。

1

2

3

主管：向下管理帶人帶心

4

193

嗯！這一批貨出了些狀況，它們還在生產線！？
In the pipeline

📱 情境對話

" *Cameron came in the office and asked Gordon questions about the status of certain products* "

Cameron 走進辦公室問 *Gordon* 有關一些貨品的狀況。

Cameron: Hey Gordon, do you know the status of these products? Are they ready to ship?

Cameron：嘿！Gordon，你知道這些產品的狀況嗎？能不能出貨了？

Gordon: Give me a sec, and I will check for you. Hmm, apparently something happened, and they are still **in the pipeline**.

Gordon：讓我看一下，嗯！這一批貨出了些狀況，它們還在生產線。

Cameron: Oh no! They are supposed to be shipped tomorrow. What is the new delivery time now?

Cameron：喔不！他們應該明天要出貨的，現在要拖到什麼時候呢？

Gordon: It looks like it will be ready in another 3 days. Let me

Gordon：好像還要 3 天，讓我看看能不能把

ask if I can expedite them, so they can ship tomorrow.

這一批變成優先處理，趕趕看能不能明天出貨。

Cameron: That will save the day, Thanks!

Cameron：這樣就太棒了，謝謝！

📖 字彙加油站

status [`stetəs] *n.* 地位、身分、情形、狀況

💡 大師提點

　　in the pipeline 就是還在生產線上的意思，正式的説法也可以用 WIP 來説，WIP 是 work in progress 的縮寫，兩種説法都很常用！在情境中，Gordon 説「讓我看一下，嗯！這一批貨出了些狀況，它們還在生產線。」用了這個慣用語。

3

主管：向下管理帶人帶心

再接一個案子！
我就知道有陷阱...哈哈！？
Bandwidth

💬 **情境對話**　　　　　　　　　　　　　⭕ MP3 92

" *Paul (technical director) is talking to Daniel (engineer) and Tom (engineer) regarding a potential project.* "

Paul（技術總監）在跟 Daniel（工程師）和 Tom（工程師）講一個可能接的案子。

Paul:	How's your current project going?
Daniel:	It's going smoothly, to our surprise none of the anticipated problems came up, so we are actually moving faster than expected.
Paul:	In that case, do you think you have the **bandwidth** to handle another project? I just got off the phone with this potential client, and

Paul：現在手上的案子做得怎麼樣？

Daniel：目前還蠻順利的，很多我們預期的問題都沒出現，所以我們現在暫時超出我們預期的進度。

Paul：太好了，那你們覺得你們還有沒有辦法再接一個案子。我剛剛跟一個公司講電話，他們的項目技術上蠻有意思的，而且做了也可以

	technically it's interesting, and plus it can boost our quarterly revenue.	幫助公司這一季的營收。
Tom:	I knew this was a trap....	Tom：我就知道有陷阱…。
Paul:	Haha I have not promised the company yet, I'm leaving the decision to you based on how much time you have on your hand.	Paul：哈哈，我還沒答應啊，我要讓你們決定，因為這都要看看你們手上的時間。
Daniel, Tom:	Okay, we will do it, but make sure to raise our bonus!	Daniel, Tom：好吧！我們可以做，不過要加我們的獎金喔！

1
2
3 主管：向下管理帶人帶心
4

字彙加油站

revenue [`rɛvəˌnju] *n.* 稅收、收入、收益

大師提點

　　bandwidth 是最近因為網路而流行起來的用語。現在很多人也用 bandwidth 來代表還有沒有空間或能力做一件事。如果我現在手上工作很滿，我可以這樣說「I don't have the bandwidth to take on more tasks.」意思是我現在沒有時間來接更多工作。

業績目標提升 15%如何！？
Boiling the ocean

💬 情境對話

 MP3 93

Martin (sales) and Sean (sales) are talking to Shane (sales manager) regarding to sales target this year.

Martin（業務）跟 Sean（業務）正在跟 Shane（銷售主管）討論今年的業績目標。

Martin:	How much of a sales increase are you expecting out of us?
Shane:	Well, I won't have you try to **boil the ocean**, so a realistic goal is definitely of interest. How about a 15% increase from last year?
Sean :	15% is a lot considering the economic situation out there.
Shane:	I will adjust your fixed income accordingly,

Martin：你預期今年要提升業績多少？

Shane：我不會要你們設不實際的目標的，比去年增加 15%怎麼樣？

Sean：以現在外面的經濟狀況，15% 很多了。

Shane：我同時也會把你們固定的薪資調整怎

How about that?	麼樣？
Martin, Sean: Okay, that sounds reasonable.	Martin, Sean：Okay 聽起來還合理。

---

adjust [əˋdʒʌst] *v.* 調整、改變、校準

　　許多老闆或主管都喜歡設定大的目標來刺激員工，但是有時候太不切實際的目標反而會讓員工失去動力，因為是不可能達到的。boiling the ocean 就是形容這樣的情景。下次老闆叫你做一些不可能的事可以用這樣回他「I can't boil the ocean!」。 在情境中，Shane 回覆「我不會要你們設不實際的目標的，比去年增加 15％怎麼樣？」時用到這個慣用語。

應該很容易，我想不到生意會跑走的原因！？
Low-hanging fruit

💬 情境對話

🔘 MP3 94

Linda (sales) and Martin (sales) are continuing their discussion with Shane. (sales manager)

Shane: About the company you visited last week, do you think you can close the deal?

Linda: Yes it should be **low-hanging fruit**, The owners are very pleased with our products, and; therefore, I don't see any reason why this deal would fall through.

Shane: Are there any other competitors that have approached them?

Martin: Yes but we offer much better product quality at about the same price, so it should be an

Linda（業務）、Martin（業務）繼續跟 Shane 剛才的會議。

Shane：你們可以拿到上週你們去拜訪的那家公司的訂單嗎？

Linda：嗯，這應該很容易。那家老闆對我們的產品很滿意，我想不出任何能讓這生意跑走的原因。

Shane：有別家競爭對手去拜訪嗎？

Martin：有，但是我們產品的品質要好很多，而且也沒有比較貴，對

easy pick for the owner.

Shane: Okay. Good let's close the deal as soon as possible.

於那家老闆來説應該不難做這決定。

Shane：Okay 很好！那就盡快把這個單子拿到。

字彙加油站

competitor [kəmˋpɛtətɚ] *n.* 競爭者

大師提點

　　正好跟上一個例句 boiling the ocean 相反，low-hanging fruit 就是形容很容易做到的事。從字面上來看是説好像水果長在枝椏比較低的的地方，所以很好摘。但是在用這個詞句時建議不要形容客戶，因為用水果形容人不太禮貌（雖然很多老外都這樣講）。在情境中，Sean 回覆「嗯，這應該很容易。那家老闆對我們的產品很滿意，我想不出任何能讓這生意跑走的原因。」時用了這慣用語。

看你上季的績效考核不是很好，有什麼可以幫到你嗎！？
Burned out

情境對話

" *Nathan (HR manager) is talking to Ashley about her recent performance* "

Nathan（人事經理）正在跟 Ashley 講有關他最近的表現。

Nathan: Ashley, I have noticed your performance evaluation from the team leader last quarter has gone south. Is there anything that I can help you with?

Nathan: Ashley 我發現你團隊領導給你上季的績效考核不是太好，有什麼是我能幫你的嗎？

Ashley: I'm sorry about my poor performance. It's just that I am so **burned out** recently because of my work here, and I don't know why.

Ashley：啊！很抱歉我的表現最近不好，我只是心裡感到有點累。

Nathan: Do you think it's related to any tensions between coworkers or just the work itself?

Nathan：是針對工作本身還是同事引起的呢？

Ashley: I get along with all my

Ashley：我跟同事都處

coworkers, and I think it's more to do with the work. I have lost the excitement that I had when I first came in to the company.

得很好，所以應該是工作本身吧！我好像失去了剛進公司時的熱忱。

Nathan: Let's have lunch together today, and you can tell me more in detail, and I will try my best to assist you.

Nathan：今天有空就一起吃個午飯吧！讓我來看看怎麼幫你。

Ashley: Okay, thank you so much.

Ashley：好的，謝謝.

 字彙加油站

excitement [ɪkˋsaɪtmənt] *n.* 刺激、興奮、激動

 大師提點

　　有沒有對日復一日的工作感到厭煩過呢？這在中文也許沒有一個特別的形容，我用心理疲倦或心理勞累來翻譯，但是在英文這個詞就是 burned out。這可以用在工作、家庭、或是對任何環境的疲倦感。

有事情是能獨立完成的嗎！
別總是旁觀！？
Get your hands dirty

💬 **情境對話**　　　　　　　　　　🔘 MP3 96

" *Rita is not pleased with the way Shawn works, so he calls Shawn into his office.* "

Alex 不太滿意 Shawn 工作的方式，所以他找 Shawn 到他辦公室。

Rita, Shawn: how long have you been here?

Alex, Shawn：你來這裡多久了？

Shawn: About half a year

Shawn：大約半年。

Rita: What have you learned since you got here, and by learn I mean which tasks can you finish completely independent of other's help?

Alex：你這段時間學了甚麼？我的意思是有甚麼工作是你能獨立完成的？

Shawn: I think I can do many things..., but probably not complete one full task without other's help.

Shawn：我能做很多事，但是要說哪一件工作是我能獨立完成的可能沒有。

Rita: You see Shawn? This is your problem. You don't **get your hands dirty** and always watch on from the sidelines. I need you to just go do it and stop letting others help you.

Shawn: Yes, Ma'am I understand.

Alex: Shawn 你懂嗎？這就是你的問題。你總是站在旁邊看而不親自去做。我要你以後就是去做而不要讓別人幫你。

Shawn：是的，我懂了。

字彙加油站

independent [ˌɪndɪˈpɛndənt] *adj.* 獨立的、自主的

大師提點

有沒有過同事總喜歡站在旁邊看但是不自己動手做呢？美國人喜歡叫別人把手弄髒，「get your hands dirty」來代表要跳下來做而不是在旁邊看！Alex 回覆「Shawn 你懂嗎？這就是你的問題。你總是站在旁邊看而不親自去做。我要你以後就是去做而不要讓別人幫你。」時用了這個慣用語。

1

2

3

主管：向下管理帶人帶心

4

這是項重要的工作，要全力以赴！？
Pick up steam

💬 情境對話　　　　　　　　　　🔘 MP3 97

> *Terry is not pleased with the progress of the project, and he called his project manager Ellen to his office.*

Terry: What is wrong? Why are we two weeks behind our schedule?

Ellen: Well, there are some technical difficulties that we did not expect. But we are resolving them now, so we should be able to recover by next week.

Terry: This is a very important project, and I want it to **pick up the steam** now. Tell everyone on the team this project is always their number one priority.

Ellen: Okay, sir. I will do that.

Terry 對項目進度不滿意，他把負責人 Ellen 叫進他的辦公室。

Terry：到底怎麼了？為什麼我們進度落後兩個禮拜？

Ellen：我們遇到了一些預計之外的技術困難，不過我們快解決了，預計下週我們就能趕回進度。

Terry：這是一個很重要的項目，我要它開始全力前進。跟每一位組員說這是他們第一優先的工作。

Ellen：好的，我會。

字彙加油站

technical ['tɛknɪk!] *adj.* 技術的、科技的、專門的

大師提點

　　pick up steam 或是 gain momentum 都可以用來形容一件事情要加強動力。steam 是蒸汽的意思，所以就像火車要蒸汽當動力一樣，一個活動或項目也需要動力。如果是已經上軌道的也可以這麼用「The project has picked up steam.」或是「The project has gained momentum.」。 在情境中，Terry 回覆「這是一個很重要的項目，我要它開始全力前進。跟每一位組員說這是他們第一優先的工作。」時用了這個慣用語。

1

2

3

主管：向下管理帶人帶心

4

喜歡這暫時角色，
不用擔責任又有實權！？
Who is calling the shots here

💬 情境對話

🔊 MP3 98

Manager Robert is taking a vacation for 2 weeks and while he's gone he appoints Annie to act on his behalf for non-major decisions. He calls Annie to his office to tell her the news

主管 Robert 要請兩週的假，當他不在時他想找 Annie 代替他處理一些不緊急的事務。他把 Annie 叫進他辦公室準備跟她講這個想法。

Robert: Hey Annie, I will be gone for 2 weeks on vacation. If there are urgent matters, you can reach me by phone and email. You get to make the less important decisions.

Annie: Cool! Does that mean I get to **call the shots**?

Robert: I have to emphasize that your authority is for non-urgent matters.

Robert：嘿！Annie，我準備要請兩週的假。如果有甚麼緊急的事就打電話或 Email 給我，不重要的事情你可以決定。

Annie：太好了，你是說我可以作主喔！

Robert：我必須要強調是在非重要的事情上你可以做主。

Annie: Sure, but there are a lot of non-urgent matters which means I can act like a boss for 2 weeks without taking on any responsibilities. I like that!

Robert: I'm glad you like your temporary role.

Annie：我了解，但是有很多非重要的事啊，就是説我可以當老闆但是又不用擔壓力。

Robert：我很高興你喜歡你這暫時的角色。

emphasize [ˈɛmfəˌsaɪz] *v.* 強調

　　如果要問這裡誰作主的話可以這樣講，「Who is calling the shots here?」當然也可以説「Who makes decisions?」或「Who is in charge here?」，但是 calling the shots 是蠻常聽到的一種説法。在情境中，Annie 説「Annie: 太好了，你是説我可以作主喔！」時用了這個慣用語。

展現你最好的實力，
我們需要高生產力！？
Bring your A game

💬 情境對話

🔘 MP3 99

Manufacturing companies usually try to crank up volume as quarter end is near to boost up quarterly revenue. Production Supervisor Charlie talks to Kirk about working overtime.

Charlie: Kirk, did you review the updated schedule I sent you? Are you okay with those extra hours?

Kirk: I notice there are 4 night shifts, and I don't think I can't make it to one of them. I forgot if it's the 27th or 28th.

Charlie: Okay Please just let me know **ASAP** so I can find a replacement. Also, please bring your "**A game**" to work in this next week as we really

製造業通常在季快結束時會試著增加產量來提升季末的營收。生產經理 Charlie 在跟 Kirk 講有關加班的事情。

Charlie: Kirk，你有沒有看到我寄給你新的時間表嗎？你能在那些時間加班嗎？

Kirk：我看到是四個晚上的班，我好像有一天不行，我忘記是 27 號還是 28 號了。

Charlie：好的，盡快讓我知道，這樣我才能找人頂替。還有這個禮拜記得要把你最好的能力表現出來，因為我們實

need higher productivity.

Kirk: Okay, I will try my best.

在需要提高生產率。

Kirk：好的，我會盡力。

字彙加油站

crank [kræŋk] *v.* 使加快…、快速作成

大師提點

我想很多人都知道 ASAP 是 as soon as possible 的縮寫意思是越快越好。這個字大概是商業用語中最常見的。bring your A game 又是一個從運動中帶到日常生活的詞句，就是要把最好的表現帶過來。

你現在要把責任推卸給其他人嗎！？
Pass the Buck

情境對話

MP3 100

Patrick is a technician in a wafer fab. He made a mistake on process and results a scrap page that worths more than 20,000 dollars. His supervisor Dean is very upset about it.

Patrick 是一個晶圓廠的操作員。他犯了一個製程上的錯誤，讓公司損失了 20,000 美金。他的主管 Dean 很不高興。

Dean: Your careless mistake has cost us. You need to give me a reason and write a report on how you will not make the same mistake next time.

Dean：你的粗心大意讓我們花了大錢。你要給我一個理由加上一份報告講說你要怎麼注意，下次才不會再犯錯。

Patrick: I am only partially responsible for this. The engineer told me to modify the recipe and I made a mistake along the way. If the engineers had modified it themselves then there would not be any

Patrick：我只應該負一半責任。工程師叫我改製成參數，在過程中我弄錯了，如果工程師自己改的話就不會有事了。

problem.

Dean: And now you are trying to **pass the buck** to the engineers? I want to see the report by tomorrow.

Dean：所以你現在要把責任推給工程師？我明天要看到那份報告。

📖 字彙加油站

technician [tɛk`nɪʃən] *n.* 技術人員、技師

💡 大師提點

pass the buck 是英文商業界中比較常出現的推卸責任用語。通常後面都會加上一個推卸責任的對象！在情境中，Dean 回說「所以你現在要把責任推給工程師？我明天要看到那份報告。」時用了這個慣用語。

1

2

3

主管：向下管理帶人帶心

4

我們可能要在新年前兩個月提高產量！？
Ramp up

💬 **情境對話**　　　　　　　　　　　　　🔘 MP3 101

" *Ralph runs a food company that produces a variety of traditional Chinese snacks. As Chinese New Year is coming, he needs to adjust his production schedule accordingly. He decides to talk to production manager Yoshi.* "

Ralph: We need to **ramp up** our volume 2 months before Chinese New Year, so we have enough inventory.

Yoshi: I have already arranged all the personnel and schedule accordingly. I sent you a copy of target quantities of different products. Please take a look and confirm if that is correct.

Ralph 營運一家生產不同傳統中式點心的食品公司。他需要配合農曆新年來調整生產的計畫。他決定跟生產經理 oshi 討論。

Ralph：我們需要在新年來的前兩個月提高產量，來確保我們有足夠的庫存。

Yoshi：我已經都規畫好了時間表跟人力安排。我發了一份產品的產量單給你讓你做最後的確認。

Ralph: Okay I will do that right away.　　Ralph：好的，我馬上就去看。

📖 字彙加油站

traditional [trəˋdɪʃən!] *adj.* 傳統的、慣例的

💡 大師提點

　　如果一家工廠想要增加產量，英文就可以用 ramp up 這個字。通常從嘗試生產到正式生產的過程都適用這個詞句。舉例來說，如果投資人問甚麼時候可以正式生產，他可以這樣問「When can you ramp up to full capacity?」。在情境中，Ralph 回說「我們需要在新年來的前兩個月提高產量，來確保我們有足夠的庫存。」用了這個慣用語。

1

2

3

主管：向下管理帶人帶心

4

推出這產品是自己打自己！？
Cannibalization

💬 情境對話

MP3 102

" *Rolling out new products are always companies' main emphasis. Ivy is aggressive in introducing good new products every half a year. However her boss Mason sees a problem in doing so.* "

發表新產品是每一家公司的重頭戲。Ivy 非常積極地每半年就發表一次新產品，但是老闆 Mason 對這種做法有點意見。

Mason: Ivy, may I have a word with you?

Mason：Ivy，我可以跟你講句話嗎？

Ivy: Sure. What's up?

Ivy：當然，甚麼事情？

Mason: Ivy I appreciate how hard you work especially in bringing in new products. However, I want to discuss with you whether such a frequent new product introduction is good for us.

Mason：Ivy，我很高興你這麼認真地工作，特別是在新產品上，但是我今天想跟你商量看看這樣頻繁地推出新產品是不是好事。

Ivy: Why not? Consumers think we are innovative and full of

Ivy：有甚麼不妥嗎？推出新產品讓消費者認為

ideas and will buy more of our products.

Mason: There are two problems I see in this approach. First, we are spoiling the consumers with so many new ideas. What if we run out of ideas next year? Second, I'm afraid similar types of new products will cause **cannibalization** with our old products. Consumers have only so much money and they can't buy old, and new products together. Let's stretch the cycle from half a year to one year and see how the market responds.

Ivy: Okay, you've got a point.

我們充滿了創意，也更願意買我們的東西。

Mason：我覺得有兩點不妥。第一，我們養大了消費者的胃口，要是我們明年沒有那麼多創意想法，那豈不是就糟糕了？第二，我們新產品可能造成舊產品的銷售下降。消費者就只有那麼多錢，他們不可能新舊產品都買。我們還是應該把每半年推一次新產品拉長到每一年一次。

Ivy：好吧，你說得有道理。

字彙加油站

frequent [`frikwənt] *adj.* 頻繁的、慣常的

大師提點

　　cannibalization 是一個商業專門用語表示說自己推出來的產品使得另一個產品的銷售下降，基本上就是產品中互相打架的現象。這個單字在行銷行業常常用到。

很抱歉講這壞消息，但是我要結束營業了！？
Throw in the towel

💬 情境對話

 MP3 103

"With rising cost of labor and rent, Florence has decided to announce the news of closing the coffee shop."

Florence: I am **throwing in the towel**. I plan to close the shop in 3 months.

Rachael: How come? Is it due to financial reasons?

Florence: Yes, I have been losing money for the past 6 months, and I don't see a turning point with the current cost structure.

Maggie: Let's think of something together! We can figure out

隨著每年增長的房租和人力開銷，*Florence*決定要宣布關閉咖啡店的消息。

Florence：很抱歉講這個壞消息，但是我要關店了。目前的計畫是在接下來的三個月中慢慢把這個店收起來。

Rachael：為什麼呢？是因為財務上的問題嗎？

Rachael：沒錯，在過去的六個月中我們持續的賠錢，而根據成本架構我也不覺得這個情勢會扭轉。

Maggie：讓我們一起想辦法吧！我們可以想

how to further differentiate ourselves to attract more customers!

Florence: I have tried everything I could think of...

Rachael: Maggie is right, let's just use this next three months to continue experimenting with new ideas. It won't hurt since we are already in a bad situation. If it still does not work out then you can still follow your initial plan and close the shop.

Florence: Okay, let's give this a last try!

出怎樣讓我們更有特色好吸引顧客！

Florence：我已經試過所有我能想到的了…。

Rachael： Maggie 是對的，我們應該就在這最後三個月中持續的嘗試。反正也不會比現在更糟糕了，如果沒有用，你就按照原本的計畫把店在三個月後關掉就是了。

Florence：好吧！讓我們再一起試最後一次！

字彙加油站

steady [`stɛdɪ] *adj.* 穩固的、平穩的

大師提點

throw in the towel 跟 give up 一樣都是放棄的意思，throw in the towel 是從拳擊的用語轉過來的。在拳擊中如果把毛巾丟到中間就是放棄的意思，而這也被普及化到日常生活用語中。

要學會聆聽，
聽出言外之意才行！？
Read between the lines

💬 情境對話

 MP3 104

" *Jonah is being promoted to manager. His boss Max is offering him some advice.* "

Max: Well Jonah I want to congratulate you first because you earned this position with your hard work and dedication.

Jonah: Thank you Max, and I appreciate your recognition.

Max: I want to offer you a word of advice on becoming a manager. You need to learn how to listen now that people report to you. Learn how to **read between the lines**. Remember it's not what they said, it is what they meant. If you cannot discern what

Jonah 被提拔成主管了。他的老闆 *Max* 來給他一些建議。

Max: Jonah 我要先恭喜你，因為你的委身跟勤奮幫你爭取到了這份職位。

Jonah：謝謝你 Max，我很感謝你的認同。

Max：我要給你一些當主管的建議。你現在有人在你下面做事了，你要學會聆聽。要學會聽出弦外之音。記住不是要聽人們講的，是要聽他們真的想表達的。如果你沒辦法分辨這區別的話，當主管會很辛

people are trying to convey, you will have a tough time.

苦。

Jonah: I will try my best. Thank you for the advice.

Jonah：我會盡我最大努力的，謝謝你的建議。

📖 字彙加油站

recognition [ˌrɛkəgˋnɪʃən] *v.* 認出、認可、賞識

💡 大師提點

溝通是一種藝術，而就連美國人這種通常表達都非常直接的，也都知道有時候人們沒法將想法全部講出來。read between the lines 就是說要觀察到那沒有在表面上的。情境中，Max 回覆說「我要給你一些當主管的建議。你現在有人在你下面做事了，你要學會聆聽。要學會聽出弦外之音。記住不是要聽人們講的，是要聽他們真的想表達的。如果你沒辦法分辨這區別的話，當主管會很辛苦。」用到了這慣用語。

試著跟他學，相信會有幫助！？
Pick his brain

情境對話

🔘 MP3 105

Jimmy has been working on down equipment for a few days but not making significant progress. Manager Art decides to call the field service Engineer to help repair.

Jimmy 這幾天在修一台有問題的設備，可是一直沒有進展。主管 Art 決定叫設備服務工程師來幫忙。

Art: The engineer will come tomorrow, and I want you to stay with him all the time and try to **pick his brain** on his knowledge about this equipment. I'm sure his experience is very helpful.

Art：這位工程師明天來，我要你全天跟著他試著學習他所知道的。我相信他的經驗會很有幫助。

Jimmy: Okay, I will do that.

Jimmy：好的，我會。

Art: Also if he wants to fix something make sure we don't just buy parts from him without checking our usual vendor's prices.

Art：還有如果他要修什麼，不要就直接跟他買零件，要先跟我們平常的供應商比較價錢以後再說。

Jimmy: Okay.　　　　　　　　　　　　　Jimmy：好的。

📖 字彙加油站

significant [sɪgˋnɪfəkənt] *adj.* 有意義的、重大的、重要的

💡 大師提點

　　pick his brain 聽起來可能很奇怪，因為白話翻譯的話好像是說拿起他的腦。但是在英文上這句話就是說要知道他所知道的，或是要知道他是怎麼想的。這詞句在這種師父跟學生的關係中常出現！

還是避免這種情況發生吧！？
Open a can of worms

情境對話

MP3 106

Denise is in charge of organizing a company trip for all employees. She intends to provide a better ride and accommodation for families with more than 2 children. Her manager Phoebe turns down this idea.

Denise: Why don't you think it's a good idea?

Phoebe: I think the intention is great, but since you have 4 kids yourself let's not **open that can of worms** and make people think that you proposed this idea for your own benefit.

Denise: That's true. It is definitely not worth it to leave room for people to to gossip.

Denise 負責規劃一個全公司員工旅遊。她想要安排比較好的交通及住宿給有超過兩個小孩的家庭。 她的經理 Phoebe 不認可這個主意。

Denise：你為什麼覺得這主意不好呢？

Phoebe：我覺得你的出發點很好，但是你自己本身也有四個小孩，所以我們應該避免這個情況，不然人們會認為你這樣做是為你自己。

Denise：也對，留給人講閒話的空間是絕對不值得的。

📖 字彙加油站

accommodation [əˌkɑməˋdeʃən] *n.* 方便設施、適應、調節、住處

💡 大師提點

　　open a can of worms 通常就是為了解決一個問題，卻又引起了另外一個更大的問題，所以用這個詞句的時候通常都是勸對方不要這樣做。在給一個示範，「By doing so you will open another can of worm, so let's not go this route.」 這樣做的話，會留給人說閒話的空間。我們別採用這個途徑吧。在情境中，Phoebe 回覆「我覺得你的出發點很好，但是你自己本身也有四個小孩，所以我們應該避免這個情況，不然人們會認為你這樣做是為你自己。」用這此慣用語。

需要時間學習跟適應！？
Learning curve

💬 **情境對話**

🔵 MP3 107

> *Nathan (HR manager) is discussing the new opening of a hardware senior engineer with Paul (technical director).*

Nathan（人事經理）跟Paul（技術總監）在討論公司工程師的缺。

Nathan: So how many years of experience does the candidate need to have?

Nathan：我們要找有幾年經驗的人？

Paul: This position has quite a steep **learning curve** and; therefore, I would recommend at least 5 years of experience.

Paul：這位置通常要上手一段時間才能適應，所以我建議起碼找有五年經驗的人。

Nathan: 5 years with a bachelor's or master's degree?

Nathan：大學生或是碩士生呢？

Paul: Bachelor is fine.

Paul：大學就可以了。

Nathan: Okay, so I will post online for a senior hardware engineer with 5-10 years of experience.

Nathan：好，所以我就在網路上發一個 5-10 年的資深硬體工程師，

Minimum education required is a bachelor's degree.

基本教育是大學以上的職缺。

📖 字彙加油站

recommend [ˌrɛkə`mɛnd] *v.* 推薦、介紹、建議

💡 大師提點

learning curve 是表示需要一段時間學習跟適應，如果這個時間很長我們就在前面加 steep， 不要用 long，因為英文字面上不是在形容時間！在情境中，Paul 説「這位置通常要上手一段時間才能適應，所以我建議起碼找有五年經驗的人。」使用到此慣用語。

這明顯是超時工作，工作量太多了吧！？
Overload

💬 **情境對話**　　　　　　　　　　　🔘 MP3 108

" *Amber (CFO) comes to Nathan's (HR manager) office to propose an opening.* "

Amber: We need one more accountant. Betty has her **hands full** now and is working late everyday especially since it's the quarter end season. Can you help find me one with at least 5 years' experience handling financial documents?

Nathan: Sure that is not a problem. But are your accountants only busy at the quarter's end? In this case do you want to consider contractors?

Amber: I think it's still good to have a full time employee.

Amber（財務長）走進 Nathan（人事經理）的辦公室提出一個職缺。

Amber：我們需要再一個會計，Betty 現在手上的工作已經滿了，每天都工作到很晚，尤其是現在是季結束的時候。能不能幫我找一個起碼有五年做財務報表經驗的？

Nathan：這沒有問題，但是你的會計是只會在季結束時才忙嗎？如果是這樣要不要考慮找短時簽約的？

Amber：我比較喜歡全職的員工。

字彙加油站

accountant [ə`kaʊntənt] *n.* 會計師、會計人員

contractor [`kɑntræktɚ] *n.* 承包商、承包人、立契約者

大師提點

　　每個人都經歷過上班上到忙到不行的感覺，當手上工作很多時就叫 hands full。但是 hands full 不一定代表工作太多，他可能是滿的剛好，如果真的要說工作太多的話會用 overloaded。在情境中，Amber 回覆說「我們需要再一個會計，Betty 現在手上的工作已經滿了，每天都工作到很晚，尤其是現在是季結束的時候。能不能幫我找一個起碼有五年做財務報表經驗的？」用到這慣用語。

要我放棄現在穩定收入，來接這個燙手山芋！？
Golden parachute

情境對話

MP3 109

Warren is going to an interview for a CEO position. Derek, the chairman of the board, is scheduled to interview him for one hour.

Derek: Your **track record** is very impressive. I was actually the one who recommended you to our company. Internally I already have picked you as the right person for the job, can you tell me what would prevent you from accepting this offer?

Warren: Coming to such an established company is like a dream come true for me; however, to sacrifice my stable job and fill in this risky

Warren 要去面試一份執行長的工作。董事會主席 Derek 被安排來進行一個一小時的面試。

Derek：你的資歷非常的出色。其實我是向董事會推薦你的人，所以我內心已經覺得你就是最合適這位子的人。你能不能跟我講甚麼事情會阻止你來接受這份工作？

Warren：當然能來到這種發展完善又成熟的公司真是夢想成真，但讓我要能放棄現在穩定的收入來接這個燙手山

position, I need to ask for a much higher compensation than what I have now.

竿，我必須要拿到比我現在高很多的待遇。

Derek: Compensation is not a problem. And your concern is legit as our board members might show a lack of patience with financial results, but I guarantee you a **golden parachute,** so regardless of your success here your personal finances are secured.

Derek：待遇不是問題。你的擔憂是有理的，因為我們的董事會也許有時候對財務報表的結果缺乏耐心。不過我給你的合約裡可以包含很好的離職福利，所以不管你在這裡成不成功，你個人的財務是有保障的。

Warren: Okay, please send me the offer, so I can take a look.

Warren：好，那請把合約寄給我看看。

📖 字彙加油站

purchase [ˋpɝtʃəs] *v.* 購買、贏得

colleagues [ˋkɑlig] *n.* 同事、同行

💡 大師提點

很多大公司的執行長被開除時拿到的錢比他們之前的薪資還多，我們稱這種高的離職待遇 golden parachute，因為明明是退場了但是拿的錢卻很多。這種機制一來是拉有才能的人來，二來也是讓他們可以安心放手去做。

最起碼要找很有經驗的人！？
Savvy

💬 情境對話   🔘 MP3 110

" *Kelvin is hiring a new marketing guy in his company. He is talking to his HR Rachael about it.* "

Kelvin 在找一個新的行銷員工到他公司。他正在跟人事部 Rachael 講這件事。

Rachael: What kind of experience and expertise are you looking for?

Kelvin: I need this guy to be very business **savvy**, so he can offer new strategies to put us in a better position. So I would say at least 20 years of industry experience. The important part is not just the experience you need to make sure the candidate has done something on the business side that helps build or save a company.

Rachael：你要找有甚麼經驗跟專業的人？

Kelvin：這個人需要非常懂商業，這樣才可以在策略上替公司有所貢獻。我會說起碼要 20 年的經驗，但是除了經驗外，重要的是必須要有做過幫助公司或挽救公司的事情。

Rachael: Okay I get it. I will get right on it.

Rachael：好的，我馬上去找。

字彙加油站

strategy [`strætədʒɪ] *n.* 計謀、策略、戰略

candidate [`kændədet] *n.* 候選人、候補者

大師提點

savvy 這個字平常比較少用，但是在商業界還算普遍。雖然這個字是像 good 跟 strong 一樣在形容很厲害或強，但是用法卻總是放在很厲害的事情後面而不是前面。我們可以説「He is very good at programming.」，但是通常用 savvy 的話，我們會這樣講「He is very technical savvy or He is very business savvy.」。在情境中，Kelvin 回説「這個人需要非常懂商業，這樣才可以在策略上替公司有所貢獻。」用到這個慣用語。

這種燙手山芋不是換個人就可以解決的！？
In the hot seat

💬 **情境對話**

> *Company is facing financial difficulty and the board decides to terminate CEO Jack and look for a replacement. CFO Benjamin and COO Sheryl are talking about potential candidates.*

公司面臨財務危機，所以董事會決定請辭執行長 Jack，另尋人才。財務長 Benjamin 跟營運長 Sheryl 在討論由誰來頂這個位置。

Benjamin: Do you think the board is looking for candidates within our company or outside?

Sheryl: I don't know, but will you take it if they ask you?

Benjamin: Absolutely not. I don't want to be **in the hot seat**. You realize that our company is in a difficult financial situation, and I highly doubt that anyone can fix

Benjamin：你覺得董事會是會從公司裡面選人，還是去外面找？

Sheryl：我不知道，不過如果他們問你，你會接受嗎？

Benjamin：絕對不會，我不想要接這個燙手山芋。你想想我們公司現在的狀況，我不認為可以請一個人就馬上扭轉這個情況。

this situation instantly.

Sheryl: Yes, you are right. I hope the board understands that, too.

Sheryl：你說的對，我希望董事會也能理解。

| replacement [rɪ`plesmənt] *v.* 代替、取代、更換 |
| financial [faɪ`nænʃəl] *adj.* 財政的、金融的 |

in the hot seat 是形容在一個很有壓力的位子，這裡用燙手山芋來翻譯是因為這個執行長換人這個轉換的過程很像換個人去接燙手山芋。但是如果執行長沒換人，我們還是可以用「he is in the hot seat」來講。在情境中，Benjamin 回覆說「絕對不會，我不想要接這個燙手山芋。你想想我們公司現在的狀況，我不認為可以請一個人就馬上扭轉這個情況。」用到這個慣用語。

該找綜合素質最好的人嗎！？
Cream of the crops

情境對話

MP3 112

Jerry calls a meeting today to discuss with the hiring manager Annie to talk about how to improve the selection process.

Jerry 召開一個會來跟人事主管 Annie 討論如何提升選擇的過程。

Jerry: We've had some inconsistent performances in these new graduates. How do we improve the selection process? I want the **cream of the crop** that can be valuable to us in the long term.

Jerry：我們雇用的學生中有很不一致的表現。我們要怎麼讓我們選擇學生的方式進步呢？我想要最好的員工，是可以對我們公司有長期性價值的。

Annie: If you want the best talent, then all we have to do is find graduates from Ivy Leagues. Won't that solve your problem?

Annie：如果你想要最好的，我們只要去長春藤或其他最好的大學找不就解決你的問題了？

Jerry: But I notice some of the best people we hired are not

Jerry：可是我發現我們公司的一些最優秀的員

necessarily from the top schools.

Annie: Sure there are always exceptions, but top schools guarantee you a minimum quality standard, so you know you won't waste your money.

Jerry: Top schools only guarantee ability, but not team work, EQ, and all the other important elements. You should think of a way to spot these qualities from interviews.

Annie: Okay, I will do that.

工並非都是名校畢業的。

Annie：當然，總是有例外得，但是找名校的學生可以保證你不會浪費錢，能有一定的水平。

Jerry：名校學生只有能力上有保障，其他也很重要的元素像團隊合作和 EQ 就不一定，我覺得你還是要設法在面試過程中挑出有這些特質的學生。

Annie：好的，我會。

📖 字彙加油站

selection [sə`lɛkʃən] *n.* 選擇、選拔

💡 大師提點

cream of the crops 一般是在形容那最好的人才，譬如說能去華爾街上班或是 Google 及 Facebook 的人。

237

客戶、股東、對手：知己知彼，百戰百勝

　　主管、同事等可以藉由慢慢相處或熟悉後習慣彼此模式，但客戶、股東或對手等則較為棘手，也不見得都能猜到對方在想什麼，在part4，我們一起來從各情境中好好學習吧。

他們不需要在這款產品上面賺錢！？
Deep pockets

💬 **情境對話**　　　　　　　　　🔘 MP3 113

❝ Kate (marketing manager) is discussing with Susan about competitor's pricing strategy. ❞

Kate（行銷經理）正在跟 Susan 討論競爭對手的行銷策略。

Kate: What are other companies' pricing trends year to year?

Kate：其他公司每年的價錢趨勢是怎麼樣？

Susan: Company A holds prices steady every year, but company B has the tendency to lower prices by 10% every year.

Susan：　A 公司的價錢很穩定，但是 B 公司每年都把價錢降低 10%。

Kate: The current market prices are already at the low end; do you think company B will continue to lower their price?

Kate：現在市場價錢已經很低了，你覺得 B 公司下一年還能再下降嗎？

Susan: Company B has a **deep pocket**, and they don't need to make money on this line of products; therefore, they

Susan：B 公司很有錢，他們不需要在這款產品上面賺錢，所以他們很有可能繼續降價來

could continue to lower their prices to put pressure on us and the others.

給我們跟其他公司壓力。

Kate: We need to think of a way to not fall into a **pricing war** with company B.

Kate：我們要想辦法不跟他們陷入低價競爭。

 字彙加油站

continue [kən`tɪnjʊ] *v.* 繼續、持續、留任

 大師提點

　　deep pockets 就是我們中文的「口袋很深」，代表著很有錢。商界中通常比較會形容公司而不是個人。pricing war 就是低價競爭，表示只能用價錢來取得優勢而沒有別的附加價值。

241

這不是麵包跟奶油是一種主要戰略或強項！？
Bread and butter

💬 情境對話

🔊 MP3 114

" Kate (marketing manager) is having a meeting with Chelsea. "

Kate（行銷經理）正在跟 Chelsea 開會。

Kate: Chelsea, remember the SWOT analysis you did last time? What was the biggest threat for us again?

Kate: Chelsea，記得你上次給的強弱危機分析報告嗎？我們最大的危機是什麼？

Chelsea: The biggest threat is the change of the market going toward low priced, decent quality smart phone.

Chelsea：最大的危機是智慧手機往低價市場移動。

Kate: And so you are suggesting Chinese companies could potentially disrupt us by offering a low price.

Kate：所以你認為中國公司在這方面可能帶給我們威脅？

Chelsea: High volume and low price is always Chinese firms' **bread and butter**.

Chelsea：大量又低價的生產一直是中國公司的主要強項。

Kate: You are right on.

Kate：這點你說對了。

📖 字彙加油站

analysis [ə`næləsɪs] *n.* 分析、分解、解析

💡 大師提點

在國外 bread and butter 是一般人的主食，而這也進而演變成形容一種主要戰略或強項的說法！情境中 Chelsea 回覆說「大量又低價的生產一直是中國公司的主要強項。」用到這慣用語。

1

2

3

4

客戶、股東、對手：知己知彼，百戰百勝

唉！這些市場都被霸佔光了！？

800 pound gorilla (800 磯的大猩猩)

💬 **情境對話** 🔘 MP3 115

" *Tim (CEO), Amber (CFO), Paul (technical director) and other executives are having a meeting.* "

Tim（執行長）、Amber（財務長）、Paul（技術總監）及其他管理階層的主管正在開會。

Tim: We need to figure out a way to push back that **800 pound gorilla**, so the rest of us can have breathing room.

Tim：我們必須要給我們自己製造一些喘息的餘地，那家獨大公司拿走太多市場了。

Paul: Their brand is so strong now that even if you make a really good smartphone you can only sell for half of their price, and that's not leaving us any profit.

Paul：他們的品牌太強，就算我們做出一支好的智慧手機也只能賣他們一半的價錢，而且不會帶給我們任何利潤。

Amber: Yes, our margin is really too thin. We must raise our price while not losing our current

Amber：沒錯，我們的利潤太薄了，我們要想辦法如何在不失去市場

market share.

Tim: I bet you this is the question that every other company is thinking about.

佔有率之下提高價錢。

Tim：我打賭每家公司現在都在想這件事。

📖 字彙加油站

margin [`mardʒɪn] *n.* 邊緣、限度、利潤

💡 大師提點

　　你工作的產業裡有一家獨大的公司嗎？在美國很多人用 800 pound gorilla（800 磅的大猩猩）來稱呼這些霸佔市場的公司喔！在情境中，Tim 回覆說「我們必須要給我們自己製造一些喘息的餘地，那家獨大公司拿走太多市場了。」用到這慣用語。

1

2

3

4

客戶、股東、對手：知己知彼，百戰百勝

打鐵要趁熱！？

Strike while the iron is hot

💬 情境對話

🔘 MP3 116

" *After seeing many app developers succeed after launching their own apps, Jason decides to give it a shot. He knows a successful app is not just about the function, but also the marketing. He comes to marketing expert Thompson for advice.* "

在看過一些 APP 開發者成功地打進市場後，Jason 決定也要寫自己的 App。Jason 知道要成功，不但 App 功能要好，但也需要好的行銷。他來找行銷專家 Thompson 幫忙。

Jason: I've got this really good app idea. I know I can finish the coding in 3 months, but I want to ask you how to advertise my app.

Jason：我有個很好的 App 的點子。我大概能在 3 個月內寫完程式，但是我想問說應該怎麼幫這個 App 行銷及廣告。

Thompson: The app world is crazy now, and it is good that you are **striking while the iron is hot**. However,

Thompson: App 市場現在是很瘋狂的，所以你打鐵趁熱是好的。但缺點是市場太旺了，

the downside is that the market is so hot that there is 2000 new android apps every day. The question is how do you expose your app? You've got to ask yourself, if your app is unique in function or if not what is the differentiation factor? I have a list of steps to do for app marketing; however, I have to warn you that to launch a popular app now is difficult.

Jason: Thanks, I will take a look at the list and try to follow it.

造成每天有 2000 個新的安卓 App 上市。問題就是要怎麼讓你的 App 突出？你要問你自己，你的 App 是不是有某一個特別的功能，不然就是有一個決定性的差異化。我這裡有一些 App 行銷的基本步驟你可以看一下，但是我必須說現在要推一個成功的 App 是困難的。

Jason：謝謝，我會看一下這些步驟然後試著用用看。

1
2
3
4

客戶、股東、對手：知己知彼，百戰百勝

字彙加油站

downside [`daʊn`saɪd] *n.* 不利、下降趨勢

大師提點

　　strike while the iron is hot 就跟中文的打鐵趁熱是一模一樣的意思。在情境中，Thompson 回覆說「App 市場現在是很瘋狂的，所以你打鐵趁熱是好的。」用到這個慣用語。

他們有改變基本消費模式嗎！？
Paradigm shift

💬 **情境對話**　　　　　　　　　　🔘 MP3 117

" *Kate (marketing manager) is having a meeting with Susan and Chelsea* "

Kate（行銷經理）正在跟 Susan 及 Chelsea 開會。

Kate: Did you keep track of all the channel sales?

Kate：你們有沒有繼續觀察所有銷售通道的數字？

Susan: Yes, and it seems like there is a **paradigm shift** in the way a group of consumers are purchasing.

Susan：有，而且其中一個消費族群好像正在改變他們的基本消費模式。

Kate: Can you be a little more specific?

Kate：能不能講得再清楚一點？

Chelsea: We are noticing consumers 55 and above are migrating to internet purchasing at a rapid pace.

Chelsea：我們發現 55 歲以上的消費者正在以很快的速度朝網路消費前進。

Kate: I don't find that too surprising.

Kate：我不覺得這很奇

10 years ago the PC and internet were too complicated for this age group, but now smartphones and tablets, and I think especially tablets have enabled older people to enjoy the Internet. I think the important thing now is how to capitalize on this information.

怪，10 年前電腦跟網路對這個年齡層的人太難了，但是現在有智慧手機跟平板，尤其是平板的簡單使用，幫助他們享受網路的服務。我們現在要想的是怎麼利用這一點來賺錢。

字彙加油站

capitalize [`kæpət!ˌaɪz] *vi.* 利用

大師提點

　　Paradigm shift 形容一種本質上的改變，不知道為什麼通常只在商業用語中聽到。像每一次科技大革命所帶來的影響就可以用 paradigm shift 來形容。在情境中，Susan 回覆說「而且其中一個消費族群好像正在改變他們的基本消費模式。」用到這個慣用語。

1

2

3

4

客戶、股東、對手：知己知彼，百戰百勝

當然是先佔先機，慢了就輸了！？
First mover advantage

情境對話

MP3 118

Kate (marketing manager), Susan, and Chelsea are continuing their discussion about older people's purchasing behavior.

Kate（行銷經理）、Susan 及 Chelsea 再繼續剛剛有關老年人網路消費的討論。

Kate: Any suggestions on how to capitalize on this information?

Kate：所以我們要怎麼利用這個新發現呢？

Susan: Even though older people are getting better at using the internet, we should prioritize on the website to give them easy access.

Susan：雖然老年人現在網路越用越熟，我們還是應該把網站做得讓他們使用起來很容易上手。

Chelsea: That's a good point. Younger people have ways of using the internet and so spending a little more time on the site is not a problem. But for older people they are likely to get lost, if it takes too long to find

Chelsea：說得對，年輕人在網路上多花一點時間沒甚麼問題，但是老年人可能就在網路上迷路了。

their products.

Kate: Okay, let's build the most old people friendly site, and hope this can get us the **first mover advantage** over other companies.

Chelsea: I think that's great because old people are usually more loyal than younger consumers because they resist change.

Kate：那我們就建立一個對老年人而言是很容易使用的網站，希望這樣子可以給我們先佔先贏的優勢。

Chelsea：我覺得這會很有幫助，因為老年人比較討厭改變，所以習慣我們以後會比年輕人忠誠。

📖 字彙加油站

prioritize [praɪˋɔrəˌtaɪz] *v.* 按優先順序處理、給予優先權

💡 大師提點

first mover advantage 就是指著那先反應的人的優勢。如果消費者只注重價錢，那通常先出來的公司不一定會有優勢喔！所以這個詞句要看情況用！在情境中，Kate 回覆説「那我們就建立一個對老年人而言是很容易使用的網站，希望這樣子可以給我們先佔先贏的優勢。」時用了這個慣用語。

1
2
3
4
客戶、股東、對手：知己知彼，百戰百勝

是該想想如過擴充
客戶群才是！？
80-20 rule

💬 情境對話

MP3 119

" *Kate (marketing manager) and Susan are talking about expanding customers base.* "

Kate（行銷經理）跟 Susan 正在討論擴充客戶群。

Susan: We should increase our customer base to lower our business risk and at the same time increase our negotiating power regarding the price.

Susan：我們應該要增加更多客戶來降低商業風險，也同時讓公司在議價上更有競爭力。

Kate: Yes I agree. Just by looking at our customer list we can see that the usual **80-20 rule** applies. However, it's hard to break out of this trend.

Kate：我同意，光看我們的客戶名單就知道一般的 80-20 慣例發生在我們公司。但是我們雖然知道，但是要逃離這個趨勢卻不容易。

Susan: Yes, but being limited to a short list of customers provides a greater risk for the company, so we should find a

Susan：是，但是清單上這麼少的客戶讓我們風險太大，我們必須想辦法擴充才行。

way to expand customer base.

Kate: Yes. Let's talk about this strategy tomorrow.

Kate：嗯！那我們明天來討論這個策略。

 字彙加油站

customer [ˋkʌstəmə] *n.* 顧客、買主

 大師提點

　　80-20 rule 是一個商業專有名詞，意思是大部分的公司百分之八十的業績是從百分之二十的客戶來的。所以一旦其中一個大客戶發生變動就會對公司的營收產生極大的影響。這是一個商業界很常聽到的詞句喔！在情境中，Kate 回覆説「我同意，光看我們的客戶名單就知道一般的 80-20 慣例發生在我們公司。但是我們雖然知道，但是要逃離這個趨勢卻不容易。」用了這個慣用語。

客戶、股東、對手⋯知己知彼，百戰百勝

我的意思是當下該把最重要的事做好！？
Nitty-gritty

💬 **情境對話**　　　　　　　　　　　 MP3 120

"Louis, Manning, and Alisa are having a meeting talking over next week's product launch."

Louis、Manning 跟 Alisa 正在為下週的新產品發表會籌備開會。

Louis: There will be at least 5 reporters on site, so we need to have everything decorated to perfection so that it looks good on TV.

Louis：起碼會有五位記者到現場，我們需要把所有的擺設都布置到完美，這樣在電視上才會好看。

Manning: Yes, and we should make sure we have enough staff on site to offer drinks so that it seems formal.

Manning：對！我們也要確定當天有足夠的人手提供飲料，才會看起來正式一點。

Alisa: Guys, I'm not trying to say that those things aren't important, but we should focus on the **nitty-gritty** first. Let's come out with the flow of the product

Alisa：大夥兒，我不是想要說那些事情不重要，不過我們當下是要把最重要的事先做好。我們應該先把產品介紹的流程安排好，然後再

introduction then pay attention to the details you guys just mentioned.

去看你們剛剛提到的細節。

perfection [pɚ`fɛkʃən] *n.* 完美、完成

大師提點

　　nitty-gritty 是一個美國人蠻愛用來形容重點的一個詞句。可能比較不正式，所以同事間私下講比較恰當。在情境中，Alisa 回覆「大夥兒，我不是想要說那些事情不重要，不過我們當下是要把最重要的事先做好。」時用了這慣用語。

客戶、股東、對手：知己知彼，百戰百勝

4

我們要改變一下這禮拜新發表會的計畫！？
Game plan

💬 **情境對話**

 MP3 121

> *Jordan walks into the meeting room with a new proposal ready to talk over with Brown and Larry.* 🞮

Jordan 拿著新的方案走進會議室，準備跟 Brown 及 Larry 討論。

Jordan: Gentleman, we are changing our **game plan** for this week's product launch.

Jordan：各位，我們要改變一下我們這禮拜新產品的介紹發表會計畫。

Brown: What are we going to do differently?

Brown：我們有甚麼改變呢？

Jordan: Instead of introducing both new products together this time, we will only introduce one and delay the other one for another time.

Jordan：把原本要一次介紹兩種新產品的計劃改成先介紹一個，另外一個留著過段時間再說。

Larry: Doesn't that mean we have to do all this preparation work all over again real soon?

Larry：那不就是說我們馬上就要再把現在做過的準備工作再做一次？

Jordan: Yup!

Jordan：答對了！

字彙加油站

delay [dɪ`le] *v.* 延緩、使延期、耽擱

大師提點

　　美國人很喜歡用運動裡的詞句拿到日常生活來用，這裡說的 game plan 就是從運動裡來的「比賽策略」的意思。拿到日常生活就跟 plan or strategy 沒有太大的區別。另外棒球裡的三振(strike out)，美國人也喜歡在失敗的時候拿來用。在情境中，Jordan 回覆「各位，我們要改變一下我們這禮拜新產品的介紹發表會計畫。」時用了這個慣用語。

提案完全不亮眼，我無法說服自己花 **50** 萬美金在這上面！？
Ground-breaking

💬 情境對話

MP3 122

" *Russel is from a VC firm, and he is reviewing Dana's business proposal* "

Russel 是風險投資公司的人，他今天在看 *Dana* 的商業提案。

Russel: Honestly, I cannot fund you from what I have seen. You either give me a **ground breaking** product, or a strong differentiation over current market. Nothing jumps out to my eyes in this proposal.

Russel：說實在的，根據你提案的內容我不能投資你。你要不就給一個技術創新的產品，要不就給一個跟現在市場差異化的產品。這份提案裡沒有提到這些讓我眼睛一亮的東西。

Dana: Yes, I know it's not the most creative idea in the world, but I believe people are the difference maker in my proposal. I have a young, talented, and passionate team that I believe will create an edge.

Dana：我知道我的提案不是最有創造力的，但是我相信團隊是使我們跟別人不一樣的地方。我有一群年輕、有才華、又熱情的團隊，我相信這給了我們優勢。

Russel: Obviously, a strong team is a factor, but I cannot convince myself to spend half a million dollars on something that I cannot measure and quantify.

Russel：強而有力的團隊當然是一個要素，但是我不能說服我自己投資五十萬美金在一些我沒辦法衡量及量化的事情上。

字彙加油站

differentiation [ˌdɪfəˌrɛnʃɪˈeʃən] *n.* 區別、變異

大師提點

在現在科技發達的世界裡，很多新創公司都要有別人沒想過的想法。美國人用 ground breaking 來形容那種很創新又特別的科技。在情境中，Russel 回覆說「說實在的，根據你提案的內容我不能投資你。你要不就給一個技術創新的產品，要不就給一個跟現在市場差異化的產品。」就用了這個慣用語。

客戶、股東、對手：知己知彼，百戰百勝

我想要挑戰極限看看！？
Push the envelope

💬 **情境對話**　　　　　　　　　　　　🔘 MP3 123

" *An energy company is rolling out its projected research plan for the next 10 years. There are a number of interesting energy sources the company would like to invest in, but they need to spend their money wisely. CEO Bill is talking to chief scientist Boris.* "

一家能源公司正在訂未來十年的研究計畫。雖然有許多能源來源選項，但是公司需要有智慧地投資他們的錢。執行長 Bill 在跟首席科學家 Boris 溝通。

Bill: Whatever our choices are, it must be a sustainable and clean energy one.

Bill：不管你的選擇是甚麼，一定要是可持續跟乾淨的能源。

Boris: I'm thinking to **push the envelope** and address fusion energy.

Boris：我在想要挑戰極限，來試試看融合能源。

Bill: Fusion! Does not that seem a little unrealistic?

Bill：融合！那不是有一點不切實際嗎？

Boris: There are recent breakthroughs that seem credible, and if we

Boris：最近在這方面有許多的突破，如果我們

recruit the right talents we might surprise ourselves. | 找到適當的人才，我想也許我們會給我們自己一個驚喜。

Bill: Why don't you write down your choice candidates and we will go over them one by one. | Bill：那你何不就把每一個可能做的項目寫下來，我們一個一個來審核討論。

Boris: Okay. | Boris：好的。

📖 字彙加油站

recruit [rɪ`krut] *v.* 雇用、聘用新成員、補充

💡 大師提點

　　美國人天生就喜歡作夢，而且喜歡做一些挑戰極限的事情。做些在當時看起來不可能的事情可以用 push the limit 或 push the envelope 來形容。

你可能要終止這個計劃囉！？
Pull the plug

💬 情境對話　　　　　　　　　　　⭕ MP3 124

Eleonore is an artist and intends to open a gallery in the downtown. She is sourcing her funds from banks and investors. Today her bank manager Neal comes to talk to her.

Eleonore 是一個想要在市中心開畫廊的美術家。他的資金來源是銀行跟投資人。今天他的銀行經理 Neal 來找他談話。

Neal: I'm sorry to inform you that you might have to **pull the plug** on this project because we could not approve your loan based on your credit.

Neal：很抱歉通知你説你的這個項目可能要停，因為根據你的信用，我們沒辦法批准貸款。

Eleonore: What is wrong with my credit?

Eleonore：我的信用有甚麼問題嗎？

Neal: There is nothing wrong with your credit, but a loan of this size is too risky for the bank, unless there is

Neal：不是針對你的信用，而是這個金額對銀行的風險太高了，除非你還能再找人來分擔。

another person signing the loan with you.

Eleonore: What if I offer my home as collateral?

Neal: That could work. Why don't you give me the address of your place, and I can run a valuation of the property.

Eleonore: Okay.

Eleonore：那如果我拿我的房子抵押呢？

Neal：那可能可以，不然你把地址給我，我回去幫你估一個價錢。

Eleonore：好的。

 字彙加油站

inform [ɪnˋfɔrm] *v.* 通知、告知、報告

 大師提點

　　pull the plug 在一般用語中是拔掉電源的意思。因為拔掉電源以後電器就停了，所以後來在商業用語中，這詞句就演變成要停止某個項目或計畫。

預計公司什麼時候
會打平呢！？
Break Even

💬 情境對話　　　　　　　　　　　　　🔴 MP3 125

" *Christine started a company making baby products for half a year. She has to present to her major investor Evan today about company's progress.* **"**

Christine 在半年前創立了一家做嬰兒用品的公司。她今天要跟主要投資人 Evan 開會報告過去半年公司的進展。

Christine: Over the past half a year, we have made steady progress in introducing innovative products that the market has not seen before. These products are gaining popularity, and parents show high satisfaction with them.

Christine：我們在過去半年成功地推出了市場上沒看過的創新產品。這些產品越來越受歡迎，而父母也顯示了極高的滿意度。

Evan: So when do you think the company will **break even**?

Evan：所以你預計公司甚麼時候會打平？

Christine: The current projection is next year when we reach

Christine：現在是預計明年當銷售額達到

10 million in **sales**.	1000 萬美金的時候。
Evan:　　Okay good.	Evan：嗯，很好。

📗 字彙加油站

popularity [ˌpɑpjəˋlærətɪ] *n.* 普及、流行、大眾化、聲望

💡 大師提點

　　Break Even 是打平的意思。通常公司都會問什麼時候打平，那通常答案會跟預計的銷售有關係。營業額的正式單字是 revenue，可是大部分的人就直接講 sales。在情境中，Christine 和 Evan 對談時分別用到這些字。

客戶、股東、對手：知己知彼，百戰百勝

通常送貨週期會因為訂的量而改變喔！？
Lead time

💬 **情境對話**　　　　　　　　　　　　🔘 MP3 126

" Aaron is calling a potential vendor for material qualification "

Aaron 正在打電話給一個未來可能合作的供應商。

Aaron:	Hi, this is Aaron from ING Company, may I speak to a sales representative?

Aaron：你好，我是 ING 公司的 Aaron，我想要找你們公司的業務代表。

Operator: Okay please hold on a minute please while transfer your call.

Operator：好的，請稍等。讓我為您轉接。

Hank: Hi this is Hank speaking, what can I do for you?

Hank：你好，我是 Hank，請問有什麼我可以幫忙的嗎？

Aaron: Hi, my name is Aaron, and I'm calling to ask about the **lead time** of your product delivery. My company ING is interested in buying raw

Aaron：你好，我是 Aaron，我們公司 ING 有興趣跟你們公司訂購原材料，我想跟您要價錢跟資料，特別是送貨

materials from you and would like a quote and terms from you.

週期。

Hank: Okay that's great. Let me get your contact info and I will send you all the necessary documents once we get off the phone. Lead time usually depends on quantity ordered, and I will make sure I organize all the information clearly and send it to you.

Hank: Ok，太好了，讓我先把您的聯絡資料抄一下，等下我們掛電話後會馬上寄給您。通常送貨週期會因訂的量而改變，我會把表弄得簡單易懂寄給您。

Aaron: Awesome, thank you.

Aaron：太棒了，謝謝.

📖 字彙加油站

raw [rɔ] *adj.* 生的、未加工的、未經訓練的

💡 大師提點

　　不管你做不做業務，在公司很容易接觸到送貨週期這個名詞。有些人喜歡用 delivery time 或是 duration。但是一般用得最多的應該就是 lead time。lead time 是從下訂單到拿到貨所需要的時間。

比一般行情的價錢要再貴一點！？
Pay a premium

💬 情境對話

🔘 MP3 127

Lisa is in charge of purchasing in the company. Bryan asks her to purchase equipment parts and gave her a link on a website.

Lisa 負責公司的採購，Bryan 給了她一個網頁連結，拜託她幫忙買一個設備上的零件。

Bryan: Hey Lisa, did you order my parts for me yet?

Bryan：嘿！Lisa，你幫我買了零件了嗎？

Lisa: Yes, I did, but the link you gave me did not work, so I had to find another source.

Lisa：嗯，我買了，但是你給的連結不能用，所以我另外找了賣主。

Bryan: Oh, that website usually offers the lowest price, but I guess maybe it was out of stock.

Bryan：喔！那網站通常是最便宜的，但是可能沒貨了。

Lisa: You are right on the price. I had to **pay a premium** for this part from the other source.

Lisa：我想那個網站真的是比較便宜，因為我後來買的就比較貴。

Bryan: I hope it is still within budget.

Bryan：希望還在預算之內。

Lisa: Don't worry. I got you covered.

Lisa：沒問題，我幫你搞定了。

📖 字彙加油站

equipment [ɪˋkwɪpmənt] *n.* 配備、設備、才能、知識

💡 大師提點

在商業用語中 to pay a premium 就是買得比一般行情的價錢要再貴一點。在情境中，Lisa 回覆説「我想那個網站真的是比較便宜，因為我後來買的就比較貴。」時用到這個慣用語。

1

2

3

4

客戶、股東、對手：知己知彼，百戰百勝

我們明天開始營運！？
Jump the gun

💬 情境對話

> *Abraham is throwing a party to celebrate his new start business.*

Seth: I love your party! Will you start running the company right away or is this just a message to people that your company will start soon?

Abraham: Oh, no. We will **jump the gun** and start the operation tomorrow!

Seth: Wow, how exciting! I hope everything goes well for you, and if you ever need any help I am always available.

Abraham: Thank you Seth and I appreciate your presence tonight.

Abraham 為了慶祝公司開張辦了一個宴會。

Seth：你的宴會超棒的！你馬上就會開始新公司嗎？還是會再等一下？

Abraham：喔！不會等，我們公司明天就開始營運！

Seth：哇，很令人興奮！我祝你一切順利，如果有什麼需要可以找我。

Abraham：謝謝你，Seth。我很感謝你今晚能來。

📖 字彙加油站

celebrate [`sɛlə͵bret] *v.* 慶祝、頌揚、讚美

💡 大師提點

jump the gun 就是要開始動起來的意思，很多人也說「let's get started.」兩種用法都很普遍。在情境中，Abraham 回覆說「喔！不會等，我們公司明天就開始營運！」時用了這個慣用語。

1

2

3

4

客戶、股東、對手⋯知己知彼，百戰百勝

理念被打槍！？
It will never fly

情境對話

🔘 MP3 129

" *Josh's company has grown rapidly and is now considered a successful entrepreneur. He is interviewed by Sunny, a journalist.* "

Sunny: What do you think is the biggest reason for your success?

Josh: I think it's about perseverance and belief in yourself. When I first started pitching my idea to VCs, most of them told me "your idea **will never fly**." But I did not give up and believed in myself. That is the main reason.

Sunny: Those VCs must be regretting that now!

Josh: I guess so.

Josh 的公司成長非常快速，現在已經是大家公認的成功初創企業家。他今天被記者 *Sunny* 採訪。

Sunny：你覺得你成功最大的原因是什麼？

Josh：我覺得是堅持和相信自己。我一開始跟許多 VCs 講我的理念時，大部分的人都說你的想法不會成功的。但是我沒有放棄，我持續相信自己，我想這是最大的原因。

Sunny：那些 VCs 一定很後悔了現在。

Josh：我想是吧！

📖 字彙加油站

perseverance [ˌpɝ-sə`vɪrəns] *n.* 堅持不懈、堅忍不拔

💡 大師提點

　　我想大家都有想法或意見被打槍的經驗吧！很多人可以直接說「It is not going to work.」也可以說，「It's not gonna fly.」或如果是比較初創的想法，可能是要在幾年以後才會看到效果的人，就可以加 never 來強調這一點，「It will never fly.」。 在情境中，Josh 回覆時說「大部分的人都說你的想法不會成功的。但是我沒有放棄，我持續相信自己，我想這是最大的原因。」用了此慣用語。

要步步為營…
外面世界就像叢林！？
Jungle

💬 情境對話

🔘 MP3 130

" *Journalist Sunny is bringing her interview with Josh to an end.* "

記者 *Sunny* 要把跟 *Josh* 的訪問做一個總結。

Sunny: Do you have some words of encouragement to share with the recent graduates who are trying to start up their company?

Sunny：你最後能不能給一些剛畢業想創業的年輕朋友們鼓勵或分享呢？

Josh: I think the most important thing is obviously to make sure you have a sound idea and believe in yourself. Another thing I want to share is to be careful of the real world. **It is a jungle out there.** Don't expect the relationship and environment to be as simple as back on campus. People will always try to take

Josh：我想最重要的事情就是確認自己有一個好的創意，然後要相信自己。另外我要提醒的就是，要小心外面這現實的世界就像是一個叢林般危險。不能用以前校園那樣的心態，因為每個人都會想要佔你便宜。所以走每一步路都要小心。

advantage of you, so my suggestion is to be alert at every step.

Sunny: Thank you for sharing Josh.

Sunny：謝謝 Josh 你的分享。

📖 字彙加油站

suggestion [sə`dʒɛstʃən] *n.* 建議、提議

💡 大師提點

美國人很喜歡用 jungle 形容一個危險的環境，所以如果你要去的地方很危險（不一定是地理位置，可以是公司、網路，只要是一個環境就可以）美國人就會說「be careful, it's a jungle out there.」。 在情境中，Josh 回覆說「我想最重要的事情就是確認自己有一個好的創意，然後要相信自己。另外我要提醒的就是，要小心外面這現實的世界就像是一個叢林般危險。」時用到了這句。

公司的市占率呈現負成長…該如何扭轉劣勢呢！？
Level the playing field

💬 情境對話

🔊 MP3 131

" *Natalie's company is losing market share to a larger firm and she is discussing this situation with Emily, her business consultant.* "

Natalie 正在洽詢他的商業顧問，Emily。因為 Natalie 的公司的市場佔有率呈現負成長狀態。

Natalie: This company has a diverse product portfolio, and they don't care if they lose money on this particular product line. How do I **level the playing field**?

Natalie：這家公司有很多不同產品，所以他們不介意在這項產品上虧一點錢。我要怎麼扭轉劣勢？

Emily: You want to avoid playing the pricing game with them because you have no chance to beat them. Smaller company versus big company is always hard, like **David fights Goliath**, but if

Emily：你要避免跟他們在價格上競爭，因為這方面你輸定了。小公司要跟大公司競爭總是不容易，但是就像大衛打倒歌利亞一樣，這個故事教我們大公司的反

the moral of the story teaches us anything it is that big companies will react slower to the market. They lack your mobility, so you have to use that to your advantage.

應不會有你這麼快。你要用這一點跟他打。

Natalie: Okay, that's good advice. I will go dwell on what I can do.

Natalie：好的，這個建議很好我會回去想想看要怎麼做。

字彙加油站

diverse [daɪˋvɝs] *adj.* 不同的、多變化的

大師提點

在情境中使用了 level the playing field 和 David vs. Goliath 時用了這兩個慣用語，其中 level the playing field 是説怎麼樣去平衡這個對立的條件。所以如果兩家公司各有優勢那這個 playing field 就是平衡的，但是如果是一面倒那就不是，David vs. Goliath（大衛打歌利亞）是著名的聖經故事，而美國人喜歡用這一個典故來形容以小博大！

4

客戶、股東、對手：知己知彼，百戰百勝

給我選的話，我會選物聯網！？
Uncharted territory

💬 **情境對話**

🔘 MP3 132

Leo and Sue are two scientists interested in the next big technical revolution.

Leo: What do you think will be the next big thing that takes us into **uncharted territory**?

Sue: This is not an easy choice because There are too many possibilities, there are the internet of things, bioengineering with the new CRISPR technology that can modify any genes, and maybe quantum computers. If I really have to pick, I would pick the internet of things because it seems like we will get there first because the others have science barriers that are not overcome that easily.

Leo 跟 Sue 是兩位對下一個科技革命的技術感興趣的科學家。

Leo：你覺得哪一個技術會帶我們到一個新領域？

Sue：這很難猜，因為太多技術都有可能，現在有物聯網、可以改變基因的生物科技新技術 CRISPR 和量子電腦。如果我一定要選一個的話，我會選物聯網。因為我們應該會先到這個階段，而且其他的技術還有一些瓶頸不容易突破。

Leo: Interesting! I guess time will tell, if your prediction is correct!

Leo：真有趣！我想以後就會知道你猜的對不對了！

📖 字彙加油站

uncharted [ʌnˋtʃɑrtɪd] *adj.* 未知的、未開發的

💡 大師提點

　　uncharted territory 就是一個未知的領域。現在的世界有很多東西都是以前沒看過、沒經歷過的。不但技術更新的快，就連汙染程度也是一直破紀錄，所以這個詞現在會很常用！在情境中，Leo 回覆「你覺得哪一個技術會帶我們到一個新領域？」時用了這個慣用語。

唉！網路書店對實體書店造成很大威脅！？
Corner the market

情境對話

MP3 133

Eva runs a brick & mortar bookstore and is facing severe competition from online bookstore. She asks Frances, a business consultant, for help.

Eva 有一家實體書店，但是受到了網路書店很大的威脅。她來請教商務顧問 Frances.

Eva: Online bookstores have **cornered the market**. My sales are dropping 5% every quarter, and it does not seem to be slowing down.

Eva：網路書店佔領大部分市場，我的營業額每個月都下降 5%，而且情況一點沒有好轉。

Frances: How much cheaper are online bookstores selling on average?

Frances：網路書店賣得比你便宜多少呢？

Eva: Most online bookstores sell 10% less than my bookstore, but it is not just the price. Most consumers now like the convenience of buying books at home.

Eva：平均大概比我便宜 10%。可是除了價錢以外現在顧客也喜歡不用出門就在家裡能買東西。

Frances:	Yes, but there are things that online bookstore cannot offer. If parents want to take kids to a bookstore on a Saturday afternoon just to enjoy some reading, online bookstore cannot do that.
Eva:	Yes! Maybe I should convert my bookstore to a kids-friendly place so that parents will take their kids there!
Frances:	I think that's a good place to start.

Frances：是沒錯，不過也有事情是網路書店辦不到的。如果今天爸爸媽媽在一個週六下午想帶小朋友去一個輕鬆的地方看看書，網路書店就沒辦法提供這種服務。

Eva：對喔！我應該把我的書店改成適合小朋友來的地方，所以父母會帶他們來！

Frances：我覺得這是個好的出發點。

字彙加油站

convenience [kən`vinjəns] *n.* 便利性、舒適、自在

大師提點

　　當一個企業或公司佔有大部分市場的時侯，我們可以說「This company corners the market.」。也有很多人喜歡用 dominate the market，但是這樣講就是比較白話的說法。

缺乏執行力跟策略思考能力就
想開公司，也太天真了！？
Go belly up

💬 情境對話

" *Isabelle is thinking to launch her own business, and she comes to Janet to seek advice.* "

Isabelle 想要開始她自己的公司，所以她今天來找 Janet 尋求意見。

Isabelle: I want to launch my own company, but I am afraid to fail, what makes a business successful?

Isabelle：我想要開一家自己的公司可是又怕失敗，什麼樣的公司會成功呢？

Janet: There are so many good ideas that **go belly up**. Many entrepreneurs lack business execution and strategic thinking. It's naïve to think that having a good idea equals the ability to open a successful company.

Janet：有很多好創業的公司後來都不見了，許多創業者缺乏執行力跟策略思考的能力。認為有好想法就能開一家成功的公司真的太天真了。

Isabelle: So how do I ensure I'm **on the right track**?

Isabelle：我要做什麼來確認我走在對的方向上呢？

Janet: First come out with a sound idea, then build a comprehensive business plan and bring it to me. I will review it to see if it's good enough to bring to a VC.

Isabelle: Okay, I will do that.

Janet：第一你需要一個好的想法，然後再根據這想法寫一份完整的商業報告。我會審核看看計畫夠不夠好去找 VC。

Isabelle：好的，我會這樣做。

1
2
3
4

客戶、股東、對手：知己知彼，百戰百勝

📖 字彙加油站

execution [ˌɛksɪˋkjuʃən] *n.* 實行、執行、完成

💡 大師提點

　　go belly up 是死掉的的意思，這句話其實還蠻白話的，因為大部分動物死掉的時候肚子都是朝上的。雖然是死掉但是也可以代表失敗，所以例句上說公司 go belly up 就是失敗的意思。而 on the right track 則表示在對的方向上。

你開個價吧！現在除了低價賣你沒其他選擇！？
Go for a song

💬 **情境對話**

 MP3 135

" As investors stop funding the company, Jack is eager to find a buyer of the company. He comes to talk to Eddie for potential acquisition. "

Jack 很著急地在找公司買主，因為目前的投資人決定不再繼續支持公司了。他找 Eddie 看看有沒有可能把公司買去。

Jack: I think I don't have a choice now but to **go for a song**. Can you name your price?

Eddie: What is the current book price of the company?

Jack: The book price is 40 million dollars.

Eddie: Okay, I will offer 20 million dollars, and hopefully that is enough for you run your company for the next year.

Jack：我現在除了低價賣你沒有別的選擇，你開個價吧！

Eddie：這家公司帳上值多少錢？

Jack：帳上值四千萬美金。

Eddie：好，那我出兩千萬美金，希望這些錢夠你下一年的營運。

字彙加油站

acquisition [ˌækwəˋzɪʃən] *n.* 取得、收購

大師提點

　　用不可思議的低價出售我們稱之為 go for a song。這種不是一般的折扣價，而是通常要有某些不尋常的事情發生才會有這種狀況。在情境中，Jack 回覆說「我現在除了低價賣你沒有別的選擇，你開個價吧！」用了此慣用語。

客戶、股東、對手：知己知彼，百戰百勝

你該扛起責任設計一套品管制度！？
Step up to the plate

MP3 136

情境對話

Victor runs a food company that sells hotdog and has been rumored using diseased pork meat. Victor claims that he is not aware of the source, but the general public has already lost faiths to the company image. Victor is seeking help with the business consultant Diana.

Victor 營運一家賣熱狗的食品公司。最近有傳言說這家公司肉的來源是有病的豬肉。雖然 Victor 一再強調他不知道來源的問題，但是社會大眾還是對這品牌失去了信心。Victor 來找商業顧問 Diana 幫忙。

Victor: My sales have dropped substantially, and at this rate my company will close in half a year. I have already claimed that this is a vendor's problem and apologized, but it doesn't seem to work.

Victor：我的營業額跌了好多，再這樣下去，我的公司再半年就要倒了。我已經說了這是上游的問題，也道過歉，但是都沒有用。

Diana: Consumers do not necessarily care if it's vendor's problem or

Diana：消費者不管這是誰的問題，因為到最

not because at the end of the day they are the ones eating the hot dogs. Now it's time for you to **step up to the plate** and implement a good system that will track the source and make sure your meat is safe before processing. This is the only way to restore consumer faith in your company.

Victor: I think you are right, and I will devise a system ASAP.

後吃下熱狗的是他們。你現在要扛起責任設計一套品管制度，確保你上游的肉在加工前是好的。這是唯一可以重新讓消費者對你恢復信心的方法。

Victor：你說得很對，我會馬上去設計品管制度。

1
2
3
4

客戶、股東、對手：知己知彼，百戰百勝

📖 字彙加油站

restore [rɪ`stor] v. 恢復、重拾

💡 大師提點

step up to the plate 又是一個從棒球借過來的專有名詞。step up to the plate（打擊者站上本壘、打擊區）轉到現實生活就是要人像打擊手一樣扛起責任，站到對的位子上面對挑戰。這個字的用法有一點像 step up to the challenge，但是又多了一份負責任的感覺。

Learn Smart! 067

學校沒教的神回覆英語 (附 MP3)

作　　者	曾祥恩
發 行 人	周瑞德
執行總監	齊心瑀
企劃編輯	陳韋佑
校　　對	編輯部
封面構成	高鍾琪

內頁構成	菩薩蠻數位文化有限公司
印　　製	大亞彩色印刷製版股份有限公司
初　　版	2016 年 11 月
定　　價	新台幣 369 元
出　　版	倍斯特出版事業有限公司
電　　話	(02) 2351-2007
傳　　真	(02) 2351-0887
地　　址	100 台北市中正區福州街 1 號 10 樓之 2
E - m a i l	best.books.service@gmail.com
網　　址	www.bestbookstw.com

港澳地區總經銷	泛華發行代理有限公司
地　　　　址	香港新界將軍澳工業邨駿昌街 7 號 2 樓
電　　　　話	(852) 2798-2323
傳　　　　真	(852) 2796-5471

國家圖書館出版品預行編目資料

學校沒教的神回覆英語 / 曾祥恩著. -- 初
版. -- 臺北市 : 倍斯特, 2016.11 面 ;
公分. -- (Learn smart! ; 67)
ISBN 978-986-93766-0-0(平裝附光碟片)
1.英語 2.會話

　805.188　　　　　　　　　105018625